INTERROGATION . . . MEXICAN STYLE

Longarm clamped his jaws tightly as he felt the gauntlet begin to compress his imprisoned hand. A quick glance told him that both *rurales* were absorbed in watching the steel gauntlet as its pressure continued to tighten.

Very slowly, Longarm began raising his left arm from his lap. He moved it slowly until it was high enough to allow him to slide his fingers behind his belt buckle, groping for the little double-barreled derringer that was concealed there.

He slid his arm upward. At the range of only a foot or two, Longarm did not need to take careful aim. He brought up the derringer, and with its muzzle only inches from Ramon's face, triggered off one of his two shots. At the instant when the red spurt of muzzle-blast was still brightening the gloom of the dimly lighted room, his second shot sounded. . . .

*   *   *

This title also includes an exciting excerpt from *Journal of the Gun Years* by Richard Matheson. Ride the Wild West with Clay Halser, the fastest gun west of the Mississippi!

TABOR EVANS

LONGARM

IN THE
SIERRA ORIENTAL

JOVE BOOKS, NEW YORK

LONGARM IN THE SIERRA ORIENTAL

A Jove Book / published by arrangement with
the author

PRINTING HISTORY
Jove edition / March 1992

ISBN: 0-515-10808-1

Jove Books are published by The Berkley Publishing Group,
200 Madison Avenue, New York, New York 10016.
The name "JOVE" and the "J" logo
are trademarks belonging to Jove Publications, Inc.

10 9 8 7 6 5 4 3 2 1

LONGARM

IN THE
SIERRA ORIENTAL

Chapter 1

Longarm was first aroused from his half-doze by the changed sound of the train's wheels as they click-clacked on the tracks. He was still blinking away his sleepiness when three short blasts from the locomotive reached his ears. The whistling was followed by the shrill distance-muffled grinding of brake shoes against the steel coach wheels and the undertone of the locked wheels sliding on the rails. The sounds diminished as the train slowed and finally creaked to a grudging halt.

Glancing out the window, Longarm blinked his eyes again, trying to adjust them to the darkness outside. Though the bright acetylene lamps at each end of the coach had been extinguished, there was enough glow from the small auxiliary lights above the center coach seats to turn the windows into mirrors. Longarm could see only a blurred reflection of his own face in the glass.

Bringing up his hands, Longarm cupped them around his eyes and pushed them against the windowpane. The improvement was small, but now he could see the forms

1

of two men moving along the margin of the roadbed, black silhouettes outlined by the lanterns they carried. The steady swaying of the passenger coach which had lulled him to sleep had ended at the first rasping noise of the brakes being applied, and the distant rhythmic chugs of the locomotive no longer pulsed through the night's blackness.

Longarm was aware that the train's unexpected stopping in open country wasn't usually part of the railroad's normal operating procedure. As he turned away from the window he slid one of his long thin cigars from his upper vest pocket and fumbled a match from the lower pocket. He was about to flick his thumbnail across the match head when the uniformed brakeman came hurrying out of the vestibule. He was carrying a lantern. Paying no attention to Longarm, he headed for the rear of the coach. Longarm raised a hand to flag the man to a stop.

"Maybe I wasn't figuring rightly," he said to the railroader. "But it don't seem like to me that we've had time to get to the Soldier Summit stop. I hope there ain't trouble on the line ahead."

"None that I'd've found out about yet," the brakeman replied. "All I know is that there's a train stopped on the other tracks and there was a signalman out there giving us a red flag. We'll know what it's all about in a minute or two, but right now I'm in a sorta hurry. I'm supposed to be at the back end of this drag."

"Sorry I held you up," Longarm said. "Looks like I just let my bump of curiosity get in your way."

With a nod, the brakeman hurried on toward the back of the coach. Longarm lighted his cigar and started to settle back. Then his curiosity got the better of him. He left his seat and started toward the front of the coach. Before

2

he'd taken more than two or three steps a man wearing a cap with "Conductor" on the brass shield above its visor emerged from the vestibule. He was carrying a folded sheet of the flimsy paper used by railroad telegraphers.

"You'd be U. S. Marshal Custis Long, I guess?" the man asked.

"You called it right," Longarm replied. "Heading for Salt Lake City on a case."

"This message is for you then," the railroader said, extending the folded flimsy. "I don't know what's in it, but we just got it off the southbound train. The dispatcher at Soldier Summit said it's real important for you to get it soon as possible without any mixup. I reckon it must be too, since the southbound train doesn't stop there unless it's flagged."

Longarm was already spreading out the flimsy. He did not need to do more than glance at the name of the sender. There was only one person who'd be sending him an urgent message, and that was Chief Marshal Billy Vail in Denver. The puzzled half-frown that had begun to form on his face deepened quickly as he read the telegram.

"Present orders changed," it said. "Get new orders from Chief Marshal Hewitt at Crescent Junction Hospital Vail."

Before Longarm could speak the conductor said, "I hope it's not bad news. But from the way that message was sent, I'm real sure it's important. It's not often we get one like it, having the southbound train flag us down so they could pass it on to you the fastest way possible."

"I'd say you done a real good job, even if I ain't got no more idea than a jackass rabbit what it means," Longarm told him. "It's from my chief, Billy Vail, in Denver. He says for me to get off this train at Crescent Junction, which is a place I don't know from Adam's off-ox. I reckon it's bound to be along the railroad someplace, but I can't recall that I ever passed through it. You'd likely know about it, I guess, because that's part of your business."

"Even if you'd been through these parts a hundred times, it's not likely you'd've run into Crescent Junction," the conductor replied. "It's off the mainline a mile or more on a spur track. And it'd be real strange if I didn't know about it because it's where one of our main shops is, besides being one of our division points."

"Then it's a pretty sizeable place, is it?" Longarm asked.

"Well, now, it's not what you'd call a big town, but it's important to us railroaders."

"From what this message says, they've got a hospital there," Longarm went on.

"They sure do. It's a company hospital, but we don't shut out anybody that needs to use it," the railroader replied. "Like I told you, though, all I know is what my orders said, to get you off of this northbound haul, get you on the southbound train, and see you get to Crescent Junction as fast as possible."

"Right now it seems like you know more about my business than I do," Longarm said. "But just tell the engineer or conductor on that other train to hold still long enough for me to get my gear. I don't reckon I'll need another ticket, or anything like that?"

"As far as the railroad's concerned, that telegram's all the ticket you need."

"Maybe I better shake a leg then," Longarm said. "So all I got to do is get my gear and step over to that other train?"

"That's the size of it," the railroader answered. "I'll watch till you step aboard the accommodation before I whistle us off again."

4

Longarm made a short job of picking up his rifle and saddlebags from the seat he'd been occupying. He covered the few steps needed to reach the waiting train with long steady strides. Just before he got to the nearest coach a man wearing the straw uniform cap that marked him as a railroad conductor stepped down from the vestibule.

"You'd be the man I'm looking for, I guess," he called to Longarm. "United States Marshal Long, aren't you?"

"That's right," Longarm replied. "And maybe you can tell me what all this business is about me changing trains?"

"All I'm doing is following orders," the railroader said. He gestured toward the steps of the passenger coach as he went on. "The Division Super said I was to get you to Crescent Junction on a redball, so if you'll just step aboard . . ."

Even before Longarm had gotten a foot on the bottom leading up to the vestibule the railroader was waving an extended arm, giving a highball signal to the engineer. Then he swung aboard and stopped beside Longarm in the vestibule.

"You'll find plenty of room in this coach right behind us," he said as a whistle sounded from the locomotive. Couplers rattled and clashed and the train began moving. "Just make yourself at home, Marshal Long. You're the only passenger we've got on this bobtail, so please yourself about where you want to sit."

"I ain't as interested in sitting down as I am in finding out what all this is about," Longarm said, bracing himself in the cramped confines of the vestibule as the coach swayed to the increasing speed of the locomotive. "You mind telling me what the hell's going on? Like how'd you know my name and all?"

"Why, there's not any secret to it that I know about, Marshal Long," the railroader replied. "Just go on in the coach and have a seat. I'll follow along and answer whatever questions you might want to ask."

When Longarm pushed through the vestibule door and entered the passenger coach he saw it was indeed empty. He glanced out of the window, but darkness was already shrouding beyond the railroad right-of-way and sealing it against examination. The only thing that he could see outside was the flickering line of light along the tracks that was cast by the coach's unshaded windows.

"You might be able to make more sense than I have about all this, Marshal Long," the railroad man said. He'd followed Longarm into the coach. Now he gestured toward the empty seats. "Don't bother about stowing your gear on the luggage rack. Just toss it on one of the seats and settle in. To Crescent Junction's not all that long of a run. I figure we'll have you there in about two hours."

"All I know about Crescent Junction's what the other conductor said. Have you got any idea why that's where we're going?"

"All I know for sure is that it's what the train orders say. But I guess I'm a jump or two ahead of you in knowing what's going on. The railroad hospital there's about the best one between Denver and Salt Lake City, so I suppose that's why they took Marshal Hewitt to it."

"Hewitt in the hospital?" Longarm said.

"He got shot up pretty bad when Blaze Brady was making his getaway from the—"

"Hold up a minute!" Longarm broke in. "I'm supposed to be on my way to Salt Lake City to take Brady back to Denver. The last I heard, he was in jail at Salt Lake."

6

"He was until he staged a getaway," the railroader replied. "Now, if you've got questions to ask, maybe you better wait till you can talk to Marshal Hewitt. I don't know any more about what's going on. All I've got to go by is train orders, and they just said to flag down the Salt Lake drag and get you to Crescent Junction fast as we could."

"Well, I reckon that's all settled and done," Longarm said. "And since it don't seem like I got much else to do than follow orders, I'll just settle back and take things easy till I find out from Jim Hewitt what this is all about."

"I've got nobody but myself to blame for what happened," Chief Marshal Jim Hewitt said after he and Longarm had exchanged greetings. "What made it worse was that the son of a bitch made me look like a plumb damn fool twice in a row."

"You mean by him breaking jail in Salt Lake City, then getting away again from you here?"

"There ain't much else I could mean," Hewitt replied. "I wasn't in Salt Lake when he busted out, but I'm in charge of the office there whether I'm in it or out on a case. Then I hustled off down here when I got word he'd been seen down at Greenriver. So I caught him there and was taking him back when he got away again right in full sight of the hospital here."

Hewitt lay stretched out on the narrow hospital bed, his shoulders and one arm covered by a crisscrossed maze of bandages. At the bottom of the bed one of his feet was suspended in a sling, with another set of bandages covering his leg from ankle to mid-thigh. His other leg and torso were concealed by a covering blanket. With his free arm, Hewitt gestured toward the bandages, a grimace of frustration twisting his features.

7

"I ought've made that Blaze Brady bastard strip bare naked when I searched him after I caught up with him in Greenriver," he went on. "But damn it, Longarm, I just never figured that he'd kept a whore's gun hid way up in his armpit where most guns are too big to fit."

"And that's what he shot you with?" Longarm asked.

"That's what," Hewitt said. "Now, those little pistols aren't all that big, but I don't guess I'll ever know how he held it there as long as he did without me finding it. And how he got his hands on it without me noticing is something else that makes me madder'n hell."

"Oh, Brady's a smart one, all right," Longarm said consolingly. "And maybe you're luckier'n you think you are."

"I'm of the same mind half the time," Hewitt said. "The other half I'd kick myself from here to the Great Salt Lake if I was able to."

"Well, you ain't kicking yourself no place," Longarm said. "And you better just figure it could've been a lot worse."

"You never got shot by one of those little pistols they call a whore's special, I guess," Hewitt said.

"I never took a slug from one myself, but I've seen a few men that have," Longarm told him. "And most of the ones I've run across were dead as a doornail, so I reckon you might say you can count yourself lucky."

For a moment the chief marshal from Salt Lake City did not speak. His face was twisted into an angry grimace as he tried to move and failed. Then he said, "Those little guns have got a four-shot cylinder, I guess you know?"

"Sure, I've seen a few of 'em myself. But I wouldn't carry one. I got a little double-barrel derringer that I keep in a little sleeve back of my belt, and it's as much gun as I need."

"It'd hit harder, I guess, if it takes a .41 or a .44 cartridge," Hewitt said thoughtfully. "But, that little whore's gun does real well." When Longarm nodded, he went on. "The first slug from the one that Brady pulled out of nowhere hit me like a mule-kick. It knocked me out of my saddle and back a ways from him. He missed his next two shots because I'd started rolling at him."

"Before you even drew?"

"Hell, I was trying to draw and roll at the same time."

Longarm nodded. "I've seen a few try that. I hate to say it, Jim, but you been around long enough to know that it don't work."

"So I figured out for myself later on," Hewitt replied. "Then his last shot took me in the leg there and stopped me. All I could do was wiggle around till I could get a hand on my gun butt."

"And you never did get a chance to get off a shot at him?"

"I got in two shots, but neither one was any good, damn it! Then I blinked out. After I'd come to, Brady was gone and there were nurses and doctors running around wild-like all over the place."

"You mean that they heard the shooting from here?"

"We'd just topped that rise behind the buildings when Brady let off his first shot."

"I'd say you're lucky you got off as light as you did," Longarm said thoughtfully. "And maybe the luckiest thing was that you were right here at the hospital."

"It sure wasn't lucky for that Jordan girl to be here. But it wasn't until later I found out that he'd grabbed her for a hostage. One of the doctors at an upstairs window saw him make her go with him. She was just riding by, I found out later."

9

"Hold on again, Jim!" Longarm said quickly. "That railroad man I was talking to never said a word to me about a woman being mixed up in this case, and you ain't even mentioned it before now."

"I still hear the bells ringing in my head now and then, Longarm. But you'd know that feeling. It's likely the railroad man didn't know everything." Hewitt's face twisted into another frown as he spoke. "I didn't find out about the woman myself until after they'd got me all trussed up. Then one of the doctors told me that Brady'd run her down and taken her with him."

"When you say her, you mean the one you called the Jordan girl?"

"That's right. Pamela Jordan. Her daddy's one of the richest men in the Territory. Owns about a third or more of Salt Lake City and a couple of big spreads besides that. He gets along with the Mormons even if he's not one himself."

"How'd Brady manage to get hold of her?"

"Now, don't ask me how or why, Longarm," Hewitt answered. "Because I haven't gotten around to finding out myself. They've hauled me around so much and poured so much medicine into me that I still can't quite think straight."

"Sure. I been in the same fix you are more'n once, Jim. I know that feeling myself, and it ain't a nice one. But whatever you can tell me can be a lot of help."

"From what little I know, Brady just happened to run into Pamela Jordan when she was riding by. I'd imagine he got a quick idea that he might be able to use her as a hostage so he grabbed her and took her with him."

"We'll leave it at that then," Longarm said. "But what I'm still wondering is how he managed to get the drop on you."

"I wish I knew myself so I could tell you," Hewitt answered. "But if anybody can run him to earth again, it'll be you, Longarm. That's why I sent Billy Vail that wire, asking him to switch you over to my jurisdiction till you catch up with that son of a bitch."

"You know I'll sure do my best to oblige you, Jim. I reckon you got some place you can point me to, where I'd be likely to pick up his tracks?"

"That's the bad part of it," Hewitt answered. "Brady's got at least a two-day start on you. And he's smart enough to cover his trail."

"Even if he's got that woman along for a hostage?" Longarm asked. "She might be as smart as Brady is, and manage to leave some kind of sign that a man can follow."

"I hope she did, but you'd be smart not to count on it."

"Now. Jim, I been chasing after crooks long enough not to do that."

"Sure," Brady said. "I wish I was able to ride out with you and not all shot up the way I am."

"Why. I'd like that too. But that ain't the way the cards fell, so both of us has just got to play out the hands we got in the deal. And you know just like I do that about all I can do is listen to however much you can tell me about this Brady fellow and start trying to pick up whatever tracks he might've left."

"Sure," Brady agreed. "But it's damned little help I can give you."

"That don't make no never-mind. You go ahead and start talking. I'll bust in if there's anything I don't catch onto. Then soon as I get all of the story straight, I'll set out after this Brady fellow and the girl."

Chapter 2

Longarm reined in when he reached the rounded top of the humpy little hill beyond the hospital. Settling back in his saddle, he fished one of his long slim cigars out of his pocket, lighted it, and surveyed the long downward slant ahead. The sun was just rising. An especially brilliant area of the sky directly in front of him marked the spot where it would soon break above the horizon line. Below him on the downslope the ghost-like thread of a trail meandered across ground that was barren except for an occasional rock outcrop or the blurred faded green of a patch of grass struggling to survive.

"Well, old son, Jim Hewitt sure did know what he was talking about when he said Blaze Brady wouldn't have much choice of a trail to take when he rode off with that woman," Longarm told himself, speaking aloud as he surveyed the rugged terrain.

"You'll find the trail east is easy to follow down to the

Crescent River," Hewitt had told Longarm before he left in pursuit of the outlaw and his captive. "Brady's got a gang of outlaws waiting for him, and the hideout's got to be handy to water. About the only place close where a man on the run can be sure of finding it is down in the river canyon or along one of the creeks that flows into it."

"I sorta figured that out for myself," Longarm said. "And it'd have to be upriver, because as I recall, there's towns all along the river south of the railroad line."

"Yes," the chief marshal replied. "And there aren't too many creeks in those parts. All you've really got to do is keep your eyes peeled and watch out for fresh hoofprints leading away from the river. They'd likely pick a place to the north of the stream. There aren't any settlements in that direction."

"Well, I've done enough tracking to pick up the signs some outlaw's left, even if it's in country that I don't know too much about," Longarm said. "And there's something else I ain't likely to forget."

"What's that?"

"Why, was I in Blaze Brady's boots, I wouldn't want to lead nobody to my hideout. First off, I wouldn't go too far before I'd set me up an ambush and wait to get rid of whoever might be chasing along after me."

"Brady's likely too smart to do that, since he's got the girl along with him." A frown formed on Hewitt's face. "She's his ace in the hole, maybe even his whole hand. But it's still a good idea to keep looking for him to play some kind of trick."

"That's what I'm hoping he'll do," Longarm said quickly. "He'd just be wasting his time and giving me a better chance to catch up with him. I need to nab him and his crew before they've got enough time to hurt that

13

girl. If I was a praying kind of man, I'd be down on my shinbones right now."

"I see what you're getting at," Hewitt said after he'd been silent for a thoughtful moment. "I guess I've been too busy feeling sorry for myself to think real straight."

"Which ain't like you," Longarm pointed out. "I got to catch up with Brady and that girl he's dragging along with him before he gets to where his gang's holed up. If I don't, she's going to be in for a real bad time. And there ain't any woman that deserves having a bunch like him and his kind going at her till she's half-dead."

"You're right, of course," Hewitt said.

"I'll be on my way then," Longarm said. "Look for me back when you see me."

Longarm stopped at the rim of the narrow canyon that split the earth a little distance in front of his horse's forelegs. He lighted a cigar as he studied the canyon's depths. Though the patches of earth that broke the steeply slanted stone face of the canyon's flank were small, he could see that others before him had made their way down the slant, for the grooves of horseshoes were plentiful. After he'd looked both upstream and down, Longarm quickly decided that if others had succeeded in plunging down the narrow rock-broken wall, he could do the same.

In spite of his decision, Longarm did not start at once. He sat for a few moments, studying the faintly marked downward grooves, more scratches than ruts, in the rock wall. Then he leaned forward as far as possible in his saddle, taking note of the trail along the riverbank below. His quick observation told him little that he had not already deduced. The beaten path between the precipitous slanting walls of the gorge held little promise of easy tracking. His brief inspection showed very few stretches of clear earth, and raw bare stone predominated on both the walls of the river gorge and the narrow shelf that bordered the stream.

In most places the rim of the riverbank nearest him was visible only as a jagged line, but after a quick inspection Longarm was sure that it provided what was quite probably the only readily passable route to the outlaws' hideout. He risked leaning forward a bit more, and now he could see that in some stretches the shoulder between cliff and riverbank was wide enough to accommodate two horses abreast.

Nudging his mount's flank with a boot toe, Longarm leaned back in the saddle as the animal stiffened its forelegs and half-walked, half-skidded down the steep side of the rocky gorge. His descent was so fast and so unexpectedly smooth that he felt no need to rest his horse. Reining the animal upstream of the river, Longarm began moving along the narrow strip of rocky soil. He soon found that the trail which had seemed so torturous from above was not quite as bad as it had looked. He toe-nudged his horse to a faster pace, and began to scan the ledge between the canyon wall and the river's rippling surface.

Unlike most of the few streams that flowed through the raw riverbeds of the area, the river at the point Longarm had reached was not a dancing stream that gurgled and sang cheerfully. Here it was a quiet greenish stream, flowing smoothly. It was deep enough to cover all but the largest humped boulders that rose here and there to split its placid surface and form a trail of white bubbles for several yards on either side. It was also a dark river, its bottom hidden by the roiling green water in most of its spattering flow.

Along the ledge which Longarm was now following there were short stretches of firm soil underfoot which held clear-cut hoofprints, and the prints gave him the assurance that he was following the right tracks. Offsetting these easy spots were places where he encountered treacherous loose rocks, water-rounded and slickened by the river's currents during its flood times. The fist-sized rocks turned and shifted easily under a horse's iron-shod hooves. In such places he was forced to let his reins go slack and depend on his mount to pick its own slow way.

Longarm also encountered areas of coarse sandy soil which were easier and quicker to cross. The loose sand was too dry and yielding to hold clear-cut hoofprints, but occasionally he passed along short stretches of very soft yielding earth where the feeble and almost invisible thread of a brooklet flowing down the river canyon's steep walls had moistened the trail for a short distance. In such places the fresh prints gave him the assurance that he was still on the right path.

For the most part, the trail he'd been on for two, possibly three, hours through the river's gorge had been easy to follow. Then Longarm suddenly straightened in his saddle, surprised by the belated realization that he'd covered a sizeable stretch of the trail without encountering any more of the hoofprints he'd been following.

Though he did not raise his voice when he spoke, it sounded very loud in the clear quiet air as he told himself, "You sure been a plain dumb fool, old son. Here you've ridden a mile or more since you've seen any tracks that was left by them two. Someplace back there they turned off this path and you weren't watching close enough to catch onto what they'd done. Now, you got to waste more time and backtrack till you find out where it was them two turned off."

Reining the horse into a full turn on the narrow trail, Longarm started back over the stretch he'd just covered. He'd ridden less than a mile, watching the trail more vigilantly now, when a gleam of white almost hidden by the scant low-growing brush caught his attention. His first glimpse told him what he was seeing. To confirm the message of his eyes Longarm turned his horse toward the white gleam and reined in.

Reaching down without having to leave his saddle, he picked the flimsy square of white from the branch where it had been draped. Now Longarm spread the soft filmy lace-bordered handkerchief across his thigh before fishing a cigar from his pocket and lighting it. Then he said, "Old son, that Pamela Jordan girl Blaze Brady's caught has got to be real smart, even if he ain't cottoned to it yet. Just as sure as God made little green apples, that young lady's figured out that somebody's bound to come looking for her, so she dropped this handkerchief to show where she and Brady left the river trail."

For a few more moments Longarm sat silently in his saddle, puffing his cigar as he slowly swiveled his head to look for signs that his conclusion was correct. Though the tracks of the horses ridden by the outlaw and his captive were scattered and scarce and the trail itself was faint, a freshly scuffed spot here and there showed that horses had gone up the sloping wall of the river canyon. Without any further hesitation, Longarm toed his horse into motion and started zigzagging up the rocky slanting grade.

To his surprise, only the first rise turned out to be really difficult. Once that hump was surmounted Longarm could see that the trail zigzagged up the slope in a series of reasonably low rises. When he began mounting them he found that by following each

17

humped ridge for a few yards his horse had little difficulty in accomplishing what had appeared from below to be a hard and challenging climb. The thick growth of bushy chamisal that had looked so formidable from the trail below thinned appreciably as he ascended.

On most of the wall of the river's canyon there was no greenery underfoot. Longarm encountered only the natural rock-ladder, the surfaces of ledges, barely covered by the hard crust of sunbaked earth that had lodged in each small protrusion, broken now and then by a few scattered clumps of paling alder-berry bushes and a straggle of brown dead weeds. However, in spite of the favorable slant, his tiring horse started to show signs of strain after it had covered the first eight or ten of the two dozen narrow shelves.

On the first wide ledge that he encountered, a bit more than halfway up the steep slope, Longarm reined in to rest his straining horse. He was high enough now to see the convoluted slant of the river canyon's walls, and to get a glimpse of its serrated rim. Nothing moved except for the occasional flutter of a clump of bushes where leaves trembled gently each time a vagrant breeze passed over.

Toeing his horse ahead, Longarm puffed out a small sigh of relief when at last the crest of the rim was behind him. He reined in and fished a cigar from his pocket and lighted it. Then he settled back in his saddle and looked across the expanse of prairie that now stretched in front of him.

Between the rim of the river gorge behind him and the now-level horizon that hid whatever lay beyond it, there was nothing except sparse, thinly-spaced, wavy desert-grass, growing in clumps to provide a stingy carpeting of the entire landscape. The grass tips reached almost to

18

the belly of Longarm's mount. The land's only feature was a distant cluster of low rounded hillocks which hid whatever might lie beyond them.

No trees nor shrubs rose above the grass; no man-made habitation was visible. It was not until Longarm had scanned the terrain in front of him for several minutes that he spotted the thin and almost invisible streak of roiled rising air which marked the location of a small fire.

"That's got to be perzactly what you're looking for, old son," he said. Again, Longarm's voice breaking the total silence seemed loud to him. Realizing that whoever had lighted the fire might be anywhere in the vicinity, perhaps even close enough to hear him, he moderated it to a lower pitch.

"Likely this stretch here is just a big mesa that that gang of outlaws Blaze Brady's taken up with has settled onto. And the smoke from that fire up ahead is bound to be where they've holed up with the Jordan girl. Now all you got to do is get her away from them."

Giving his horse a nudge with the toe of his boot, Longarm let the animal pick its own way across the grassy expanse that lay between him and the wavering hazy column of rising hot air. He divided his attention between the terrain directly in front of him and the distant sweep of the jagged horizon. As always he swept his eyes from side to side, and he stopped for a moment to study the shimmering and almost invisible heat line that marked his goal.

Longarm had covered a bit more than a mile when he saw the tip of a stovepipe breaking the jagged horizon line. He reined in at once and for a moment sat in the saddle studying the ground in front of him. The only cover it afforded was the grass clumps. Reining in, he dismounted and dropped the reins of his horse to dangle from its bridle. He reached for his rifle in its saddle scabbard, pulled it free, and started toward the spot where the tip of the stovepipe rose.

With each step Longarm took, the stovepipe seemed to grow longer. When he'd covered a half-dozen paces the straight line of a roof's gable showed, an alien form on the jagged broken horizon. Longarm dropped to the ground and flattened out. He closed his hand around the forestock of his rifle and began crawling on all fours as he resumed his slow, careful progress.

Lower on the ground now, Longarm could no longer see the stovepipe, but he'd marked its location into his memory, and after he'd advanced on a short distance, the top of the pipe once more came into sight. He guided himself by it to be sure that he would keep moving in a straight line. He'd covered what seemed to be a long stretch of ground in his slow but steady progress when he heard the crunch of boot soles on the hard ground ahead of him.

Stopping his advance and hugging the ground, Longarm strained his ears to hear any noise that might give him an idea of what he was running into. He did not have long to wait. He'd just halted when a man's voice broke the silence ahead of him.

"Squinty and Murphy's getting itchy, Blaze," the unseen man said. "They been just about slobbering on theirselves every time they look at the woman in there."

"And I don't guess you're much different, are you, Kelly?" The rasping voice was that of another man.

In his improvised place of concealment Longarm waited for the reply that might guide the course of action he was already planning. He risked raising his head to get a quick look at the two outlaws as well as to examine their hideout. From his present position he could see not only the men, but the knocked-together shanty that rose in the little saucerlike depression beyond them.

Blaze Brady was standing with his back half turned to Longarm, but was instantly recognizable. Longarm had had dealings with him before. Longarm had never seen the man called Kelly; the outlaw's face was not fully visible. Like Brady, Kelly wore a checked shirt and Levi's jeans. Brady was the bulkier of the pair. He had broad shoulders and was clean-shaven. The second outlaw sported a grizzled two-or three-week beard. His nose was hooked like that of a hawk, and since he was hatless with no brim to shade his face, Longarm could see the glint of his cold blue eyes.

Kelly was rolling a cigarette, and Brady stood silent until his companion's smoke was licked along its length and tucked into his mouth. While he began to light the cigarette, Longarm took the moment or two of silence between the pair to take stock of the outlaws' shelter.

It was not a place that Longarm would have occupied by choice. Its walls and roof had been made from bits and scraps of weather-beaten lumber with metal store-front signs covering a few sections of its walls. Both the single window and the door in the wall facing him were badly out of plumb and open to the elements. The rooftree sagged in its center, and the round tin chimney rising from the roof was canted at such a sharp angle that it looked as though it might fall any moment. When he saw Kelly had finally lit his smoke, Longarm returned his full attention to the pair.

"Well, damn it, Blaze," Kelly said, "a man's got to get outa this place for a little spell once in a while. Now, I guess it's different with you, because you been into town a time or two."

21

"So what if I have?" Brady demanded. "You and Squinty and Murphy have got your faces on wanted posters all over everyplace. I'm the one that's had to go in town to buy grub."

"That's right enough, but what about it? All that means is that the rest of us has been stuck here, and until you showed up with this gal you've brought in tow, it'd been a while since me and Squinty and Murphy'd even seen a woman. It sure seems to me like as long as we got that Jordan girl, we might as well go ahead and have ourselves a little bit of fun with her."

"Now, you listen to me, Kelly," Blaze Brady replied. "That Jordan girl you're talking about just might be worth a lot more than just a wham-bam-thank-you-ma'am. Her old man's so damn rich that he can pay about any price we ask to give her back to him."

"You're talking about kidnapping and ransom now, Blaze. And I've heard you say yourself that the lawmen and judges in Utah Territory is hell on wheels about a woman that even gets her chin chucked by anybody except her husband. No, sir! When we get through with her, she's going to be dead meat and we'll bury her where nobody's likely to find her grave. Me and Squinty and Murphy don't aim to climb them gallows steps."

"Well, you're damn fools if you pass up this chance to get a stake big enough to let all of us lay low for a while," Brady snorted. "Why, with what we'd get for her ransom we could go to someplace a good ways from here where there's no want out for us and live like nabobs for a long time. I got a sorta hankering to have a chance to get fat and sassy for a change."

"And how long do you figure we'd last in a town?" Kelly demanded. "If her family's rich as you say it is, they'll be putting up wanted posters from here to Hell's half acre. Then the first thing you know some half-assed lawman's going to spot us and we'll be slammed in the lockup again."

While listening to the outlaws, Longarm had taken advantage of their preoccupation to edge closer to the hideout. There was little cover between him and the building, and he was sure that they'd spot his movement when their argument lost its steam. But his slow careful advance had not yet been noticed, and he was reaching for his Colt to throw down on the two renegades when a muffled scream, smothered quickly, sounded from the cabin.

"Looks like Murphy and Squinty's got tired of waiting," Brady said. "Come on. We better go in and show 'em how the hog et the cabbage."

"Damn right!" Kelly agreed. "I don't mind cutting cards for turns, and I'll take whatever one I draw, but I ain't going to let them two yahoos wear out that gal before I get at her, not unless they get luckier than I do!"

Both Blaze and Brady and Kelly pushed through the door and disappeared into the cabin. Longarm wasted no time. He hurried toward the ramshackle structure, and reached it just as loud voices raised in argument burst out inside.

Chapter 3

None of the men in the cramped gloom of the little one-room cabin noticed Longarm come through the door. There were four of them, crowded into the narrow space between the two beds which stood in the back corners of the room. All of them were totally absorbed in their struggles, all silent except for an occasional oath and the gasping of their breathing. Locked man on man, they swayed back and forth, straining their intertwined arms, shuffling their feet to avoid being thrown to the floor.

Until Longarm's eyes adjusted to the half darkness, all that he could see was the blurred moving figures of the outlaws shuffling in their tight cluster. He also saw Pamela Jordan outlined against the bare mattress of one of the beds. The way in which she was lying, with her arms outstretched above her head and her legs spread to the bottom corners of the bedstead, told him that her ankles and wrists had been lashed to the bedposts.

During the few seconds required for Longarm to make his eye-flicking survey of the cabin's interior, the fracas at the back of the room had continued. Suddenly Blaze Brady's voice rose above the bubble of half shouts and oaths.

"I get first go at her, damn it!" he said. "I'm the one that brought her here!"

"Hadn't been for Kelly and Murphy and me, you wouldn't've had no hidey-hole to take her to!" one of the other men said hotly. "This here's our place, so it's got to be one of us that gets her first!"

"Squinty's right!" another agreed. "You're at the tag end of the four of us, Blaze. Now, be square about it and let's quit wrangling thisaway."

"There ain't but one fair way to settle things," Kelly suggested. "That's cutting cards to see who'll be the first!"

"Damned if I'll settle for that!" Brady exclaimed. "I'll fist-fight you one at a time or all in a bunch before I give ground!"

Longarm's eyes had now adjusted fully to the semi-darkness of the cabin's interior, but the only members of the gang he could identify with any certainty were Brady and Kelly. The outlaws had continued their pushing and pulling at one another while they argued, but none of them appeared to be hurting. Longarm could see that their present behavior must be the commonplace method they used to settle disputes.

He also realized that their scuffle was self-defeating. Brady was grasping one of his adversary's wrists with one hand while the fingers of both men's other hands were interlocked as they swayed and shuffled in an effort to gain an advantage. Kelly was behind the fourth man, balancing on outspread legs, his hands clamped on the elbows of his struggling opponent, who was twisting and squirming in an effort to break free.

None of the four was in any better position than his adversary, and all of them were so engrossed in their individual see-sawing struggles that they were still unaware of Longarm's presence. Now, with his eyes finally adjusted to the semi-darkness, Longarm took a moment to look more closely at the woman on the bed. As he'd realized from his first quick look, her arms were stretched above her head, her wrists lashed to the brass bars of its headstead, and her ankles secured to the foot with short lengths of rope. A bandana tied around her mouth kept her from speaking, but her head was turning and her eyes were flicking as she tried to watch both pairs of scuffling outlaws.

Longarm wasted no time in trying to stop the fracas with words. He kept his eyes on Blaze Brady, sure that if he could corral the ringleader, the others would give up quickly. He watched for his chance. When Brady stepped back, his right arm dropping to set up another roundhouse swing at his opponent, Longarm took the single long step needed to bring him to the outlaw leader's back.

Brady launched his blow at the man he was fighting. It landed squarely on his antagonist's jaw. The outlaw's eyes rolled up in their sockets to show a strip of white as he dropped to the floor of the hut and lay motionless. Brady sidled back, his feet outspread, his arms hanging at his sides, looking down at the outlaw he'd felled. It was obvious that the renegade was still unaware that Longarm had entered the cabin.

Stepping within easy reach of the outlaw's back, Longarm holstered his Colt and pulled his handcuffs from the loop on the back of his belt. He grabbed one of Brady's dangling wrists and snapped one of the cuffs onto it. Then he braced himself as Brady began to turn around at the feel of the cold steel shackles, and grasped the outlaw's free wrist before Brady had time to start a swinging blow. At the same time Longarm twisted the handcuff he still held, applying a cutting pressure to the manacled wrist until Brady was forced to bend and half turn in an effort to ease its painful bite.

Longarm got a bit of unexpected help as the man Brady had felled started to get up. The downed outlaw reached for Brady and managed to get hold of his sleeve. The tugging of the outlaw trying to stand up pulled Brady's free arm down to the level of the already attached shackle, and Longarm quickly snapped the second wristlet closed to hold Brady's arms behind his back.

Brady had recognized Longarm by now. He shouted, "What the hell! Longarm! Where'd you come from?"

Longarm did not bother to reply. In the narrow cramped rectangular enclosure formed by the two beds, Kelly and his adversary were still swapping blows. If they'd heard Brady's shout they gave no evidence of it, but continued their toe-to-toe slugging match. Longarm tilted his Colt upward and fired a shot through the roof. The crack of the shot set echoes reverberating in the little room and stopped the fracas in an instant. When the outlaws turned, seeking the source of the shot, they found themselves staring into the muzzle of Longarm's leveled revolver.

"Get your hands up over your heads and stand still!" Longarm ordered them.

He began swinging the muzzle of his Colt in short arcs from side to side. The man who'd been lying on the floor started struggling to his feet, and Longarm took a half step back to put an extra bit of space between himself and the outlaw. For a moment the renegade stood swaying groggily. Then he saw Longarm's Colt covering the group. Wordlessly accepting defeat, he hesitated for only a few seconds before reluctantly raising his arms and stepping up to stand beside the others.

"Maybe some of you men don't know who I am," Longarm went on. "So I'll do everything legal and proper. My name's Custis Long. Deputy United States marshal. And I'm putting all of you under arrest."

"Like hell you are!" Brady snapped. "You got to prove we broke the law before you can arrest us!"

"Why, Brady, you're too old a hand at outlawing to figure you can go free by pulling a flimsy bluff like that one," Longarm told him. "Not that I blame you for trying. Now, I want you men to behave yourselves. I'd as lief shoot you where you stand, but I got a duty to the law, so you can count on getting a fair trial before you get sent off to the Federal pen."

A rustling sounded from the bed where Pamela Jordan lay bound and gagged. Longarm stepped over and loosened the gag, then began working on the ropes.

"Thank goodness!" Pamela sighed after she'd taken a deep breath. "I was afraid you weren't ever going to get around to untying me. I've been here listening to those men talking about what they intended to do with me for what seems to me a very long time."

"Well, ma'am, I wasn't aiming to let you stay there any longer'n I could help," Longarm told her. "But I figured you'd know I had to corral these outlaws first. I reckon you'd be Miss Pamela Jordan?"

"How did you know my name?" she asked. "I don't recall ever having seen you before."

"That's on account of I work outa the Denver marshal's office, Miss Jordan. I was on my way to Salt Lake City when my chief wired me to stop at Crescent Junction and give the Utah Territory marshal a hand. That's because he'd taken a slug in the leg while he was bringing in this Blaze Brady fellow."

"I understand," she said. "But I'm sure you can see that I'm terribly uncomfortable tied up this way. Could you let these outlaws just stay where they are until you've freed me?"

"Why, sure. I was figuring on doing that, but I just hadn't got around to it yet," Longarm said. "Now, I'll get out my pocketknife to cut you loose. I'll be obliged if you'll keep an eye on these renegades and yell if any of 'em so much as winks his eyes. If I cut them bindings off of one hand, can you do the rest of getting loose?"

"Of course. And I'll watch these men at the same time. If one of them makes even the slightest move, I'll warn you."

Longarm managed to get the blade of his clasp-knife open without having to move his gun hand. He sawed through the thongs that bound one of Pamela Jordan's hands while still holding the outlaws in check with the threat of the leveled Colt. When Pamela had pulled away the rest of the ropes that had bound her, she stood up with a sigh of relief.

"I don't suppose I'll ever be able to thank you enough for getting me away from these men," she told Longarm. "I don't usually feel afraid, but this is one time when I did."

"There ain't no reason for you to worry now," Longarm assured her. "And now I know you're all right, I better get their guns away from that bunch. I reckon you know how to handle a pistol?"

"My father started teaching me how to shoot when I was about ten years old," she said with a smile. "And I've kept in practice."

"Good," Longarm said. "I'll pass one of their guns on to you, and you can keep 'em corraled while I see about getting the horses ready. If we don't do a lot of lallygagging, we'll have plenty of time to get back to Crescent Junction, even if we have to make the last mile or two in the dark."

"You know, Longarm, I don't see how you managed to get Pamela Jordan back and capture those outlaws at the same time," Jim Hewitt said after listening to Longarm's abbreviated account of his day's work. "I expected you'd have to look for her three or four days. Maybe even a week or more, you not knowing the country hereabouts."

"Why, Jim, it wasn't such a much," Longarm replied. "That fool Blaze Brady left a trail a blind man could follow. And Miss Jordan helped a lot. She managed to leave her handkerchief for a marker where they'd turned off the main canyon trail on their way to the place where his friends in that outlaw gang were holed up. I cottoned right off to why she'd left it, and rode right up to their little shack."

"Well, the ruckus Brady raised certainly didn't do him any good," Hewitt said. "And now that you've got him, I suppose you'll be starting out pretty soon to take him back to Denver?"

"The only reason I was heading for Salt Lake City was to take custody of him and haul him to Denver so's he could keep that date he's got with the hangman," Longarm said.

"Then I'll save you the trouble and send Billy another wire to tell him you're on your way and bringing Brady with you," Hewitt said. "And I'm sure that Billy'll see that outlaw gets what he deserves after you've delivered him."

"Then I reckon the easiest thing to do is just turn around right here and head back with him," Longarm said. "I've got some days off coming, so when I get back to Denver I don't figure to do much of anything. It's been a while since I had time to loaf around a mite."

"You can start loafing right now, if that's what you feel like doing," Hewitt told him. "The hospital's got two or three bedrooms complete with bathtubs and running hot water that they keep for relatives visiting patients. I've spoken for one of them for you to use until the next train for the main line pulls out."

"Well, thanks, Jim. I hadn't even begun to think about where I was going to stay here."

"After the help you've been, I sure don't want you to feel cramped up or uncomfortable while you're waiting to get back to Denver."

"Now, that's real thoughtful of you," Longarm said. "A good hot bath and a full night's sleep is what I need right now. So, I'll just mosey along and soak in the bathtub for a while. Then tomorrow you and me can figure out how much red tape I got to unwind before I can be on my way."

Longarm had gotten halfway from the chief marshal's room to the central corridor before he remembered that Hewitt had forgotten to give him directions to the room he'd be occupying. Deciding that it would be easier to take the few additional steps to the reception desk and inquire there, he went on to the end of the hall. As he turned into the main hallway he almost collided with Pamela Jordan, who was stepping away from the reception desk.

"Why, Marshal Long!" she said. "I hope you're not getting ready to leave so quickly."

"No, I just come down here to get the key to a room in the hospital that Chief Marshal Hewitt fixed up for me to have."

From behind the reception desk the clerk said, "I have it for you right here, Marshal Hewitt said you'd be picking it up."

As he spoke, the clerk slid a key across the counter. Longarm pocketed it with a nod of thanks. When he turned away from the counter, Pamela spoke up. "I'll be glad to show you where your room is, Marshal Long. I'm on my way to my room, and I'm sure we'll be neighbors, because there's only one section of the hospital reserved for visitors."

"That's a real nice offer," Longarm told her. "It'll sure beat having to prowl all over in a big place like this. But I guess I better tell you, if it's all the same to you, I'd as lief be called Longarm as Marshal Long. It's friendlier, most of the time."

"Yes, of course," Pamela said. Then as they started down the corridor she said, "You're going to be around for a while, I hope?"

Longarm shook his head. "Not likely. I've got to take that outlaw I come for back to Denver. He cheated the hangman once, even if it wasn't for very long, so I need to get him back there just as quick as I can."

"Do you know when you'll be leaving?"

"I figure tomorrow, next day at the latest."

"Oh, that's too bad!" Pamela exclaimed. "I was intending to invite you to our family ranch for a few days. It's only a half-day ride, and I'm sure my father would like to thank you for getting me away from those outlaws."

"I'd be pleased to get acquainted with him," Longarm replied. "Not to get thanked for just doing my job, but

32

so's I could get a few days' rest. The way it is now, I'll likely be leaving tomorrow."

"From what I overheard those outlaws saying, he's a really bad badman, if I'm not just repeating myself."

"He's one of the worst ones," Longarm agreed. "His wanted sheet's got a dozen killings on it and maybe two or three times as many holdups."

Longarm and Pamela had been moving steadily along the door-lined corridor as they chatted, and now she indicated the entry of a hallway branching off it. "Our rooms are just a few doors down. I've stayed in one of them before, and they're not fancy, but they are comfortable."

"Well, I've slept on the ground enough so nothing much bothers me," he told her. "I'll soak in a hot bath a little while, then I'll drop down on the bed and sleep like a log."

"Oh, so will I," Pamela agreed. "And maybe we'll run into one another in the morning before you leave. So let's just say good night instead of good-bye."

"Sure," he nodded. "Good night, Pamela."

"And good night to you, Longarm."

In the room that Longarm entered the furnishings were spartan but adequate: a double bed, two chairs, and a small table with a mirror hanging above it. Through a door which stood ajar at one side he saw the curving bend of an oversized bathtub. Dropping his gear to the floor, Longarm deferred locking the door while he went into the bathroom and pushed the stopper into the drain, then juggled the hot and cold faucets until the temperature of the flow satisfied him.

Stepping back into the bedroom, he stripped quickly and returned to the bathtub. It was filling nicely, and Longarm did not even consider waiting, but stepped into

33

it and lay back to relax as the warm water crept slowly up to cover him. He closed his eyes, and was relishing a luxury he hadn't been able to enjoy for several days when he heard the click of his room's door.

Surprised, certain that he'd locked the door, he popped his eyes open and sat up in the tub. Pamela Jordan was standing in the doorway. She wore a lounging robe. She said, "I didn't mean to startle you, Longarm. I was just about to begin filling the tub in my room when I realized I'd much rather join you in yours. I hope you don't mind."

"There's one thing I never learned to do, Pamela," he told her. "And that's to say no to a pretty lady."

Even before Longarm had finished speaking, Pamela was shrugging out of the robe she had on. It dropped to the floor, and Longarm felt his groin responding as he looked at her slim symmetrical naked figure. Her skin was clear and flawless, the budded tips of her bulging breasts a light crimson. Below generous hips the sparse vee of her pubic brush glistened darkly between shapely thighs.

Moving up to the bathtub, Pamela stepped in and lowered herself into the warm water to sit facing Longarm. She said, "You must've been surprised when you saw me come in."

"Oh, I was," Longarm said. "But it's the nicest surprise I've had since I got here."

Pamela's fingers were at Longarm's crotch now, caressing his erection. "And now you're surprising *me*. It's such a pleasing surprise that I don't want to wait until we've bathed and dried off."

"Then don't," Longarm said. "Because I reckon I'm about as anxious to get started as you are."

Wasting no more time in conversation, Pamela levered herself up and crouched above Longarm. She lowered her hips slowly until she'd reached down between her thighs to place him, then with one quick falling move dropped to take in his full erection.

A gasp of pleasure burst from her lips. She rocked back and forth for several moments, then let her full weight rest on Longarm. After a moment or two of motionlessness, she began rocking back and forth in a slow steady rhythm and rotating her hips as she swiveled them from side to side.

Longarm caught her rhythm and began bringing his own hips up to meet her downward moves. After several minutes had passed Pamela stopped her slow gyrations. Longarm understood her unspoken suggestion. Clasping his arms around her, he stood up, bringing her with him. Pamela locked her legs around his hips to keep him buried, then clung tightly as he stepped out of the cramped bathtub and carried her to the bed.

When Longarm reached the bed's edge he leaned forward to let Pamela's weight drag them down. As he fell atop her he drove even more deeply than before. Pamela gasped, a cry of pleasure. Without interrupting Longarm's steady thrusts she started twisting her shoulders from side to side, rubbing the firmly budded tips of her generous breasts against the wiry matted curls on his chest.

Their rhythmic coupling seemed endless, but at last the moment arrived when Pamela's body started trembling in quickly moving spasms. Longarm caught the change and began driving faster. Pamela continued to tremble, spastic shudders breaking the rhythm of her response to Longarm's drives, until at last her rhythm broke and shudders swept her while joyful sobs broke from her lips.

Longarm was reaching completion now. He had driven until Pamela began shuddering, then arched his back and increased the tempo of his thrusts until Pamela's cries of joy had broken the stillness. Now he reached his peak and passed it, then held himself motionless during the final spasmic thrusts of his completion. When Pamela's tremors had passed he allowed himself to relax, and they lay quietly motionless in the stillness of the dark room.

Pamela broke the silence. She said, "You've certainly got a way of pleasing a woman, Longarm. I feel fine right now, but I hope it won't be too long before we do it again."

"You don't have to worry about that," Longarm assured her. "I was wondering how long it'd be till you'd be ready again."

"Then don't wonder any longer," she told him. "The sooner the better. Right now's the best time I can think of."

Chapter 4

Longarm walked along the wide dark corridor on the second floor of the Denver Federal Building with the assured strides of a man who was thoroughly familiar with his surroundings. Carrying his saddlebags and rifle, he headed toward the only patch of light that broke the hallway's gloom, a luminous rectangle that glowed through the translucent etched glass of a door panel. He stopped when he reached the door where the light from inside silhouetted the glass and brought out in gold-leaf letters the words "United States Marshal, First District Court of Colorado."

Opening the door, Longarm stepped into dimness of the familiar reception room. As he'd been sure would be the case, the glow of dim light which was spilling into the corridor from the big chamber came from the half-opened door of the chief marshal's private office at one side of the reception area. Before Longarm could start toward the open door Billy Vail's voice broke the silence.

"Come on in, Long," Vail called. "I've been waiting for you."

"How'd you know—" Longarm began as he started toward the door of Vail's office.

"Jim Hewitt sent me a wire the day you left to come back so I knew you'd be getting here either today or tomorrow, and you always stop in on your way home from the depot when you get back from working a case."

"I guess I better tell you right off why I made it today," Longarm said as he reached the door of the chief marshal's office. "I got me a berth in one of them fancy Pullman cars that was hitched to the night express outa Salt Lake. It cost more'n a day coach, but I figured you'd understand that I was due a chance to catch up on the sleep I'd lost while I was giving Marshal Hewitt a hand."

By the time Longarm finished his explanation he was in Vail's office. The chief marshal waited to reply until Longarm had settled into the red plush upholstered chair that he favored.

"I guess you got as rested up on that trip as a man could expect to do," Vail told him. "But don't start getting any ideas about poker games or pretty women now that you're back here in Denver. I've got a case waiting for you, so you'll be turning around and starting out again just as soon as you can get ready."

"Now you hold on just a damn minute, Billy!" Longarm protested. "Seems like to me like you oughta have some nice little simple case I can take on, one I can work outa the office here and not have to do a bunch more traveling right off. It'd be a real fine feeling just to sleep in my own bed for a change, and have a little spell that'd sorta give me time to catch my breath."

38

"I figured that's about what you'd be looking for," Vail said. "And I hate to disappoint you. The thing is, I've already got your name on a case that's going to take you outside of the district again."

"Again means right away, I take it?"

"As soon as you can get ready. You ought to be able to leave for Monterrey within the next couple of days."

"Monterrey?" Longarm frowned. "How come not Mexico City?"

"Monterrey," Vail repeated. "That's where most of the gold in Mexico's mined, and it's far enough away from Mexico City so that this gold-thieving gang can work without having some high muckety-muck looking over their shoulder."

"I reckon that makes sense," Longarm said. He was silent for a moment. "Not that I'm complaining, Billy, but I don't guess you'd mind telling me why you're setting me to travel again so soon?"

"By now you ought to know it's because I can trust you to close your cases, Long. That counts a lot with me, even if you generally manage to spend more than your expense allotment and always seem to play more hell with rules and regulations than any other deputy working out of this office."

"There's times when I don't know whether you're telling or asking, Billy," Longarm observed after a short spell of silence. "So why don't you tell me about this new case? Or had you rather wait till just before I start out?"

Vail frowned thoughtfully for a moment, then he said, "I guess you've had breakfast?"

"I stopped at the depot restaurant and had me a bite."

"Then I'll do it now, while everything's still quiet out there in the office."

While he and Vail were talking, Longarm had taken out one of his long slim cigars. He flicked his iron-hard thumbnail across a match to light the cheroot, and settled more comfortably into his chair while Vail opened the bottom drawer of his desk and took out a fat sheaf of papers that bulged in their manila folder.

"This case isn't just chasing after a bunch of trigger-happy outlaws," the chief marshal explained. "You'll be running into some of the smartest, meanest men in Mexico with nobody around to back you up."

Longarm leaned forward in his chair. "If I didn't know better, I'd figure you'd just be joshing me, Billy. When one of us marshals is working a case along the border, you're the one that's always telling us to be sure and stay on our side."

"This is one time when you won't hear me say that," Vail promised. "Damn it, Long. You know that what you do in the field always depends on what kind of case you're working."

"Sure. And you know I'm just joshing, Billy. Go on and tell me about this new case. Monterrey, you said?"

"You'll need to start from Monterrey. It's down south from the border in what they call the Sierra Madre Oriental."

"I don't know all that much about Mexico, Billy, but ain't I right about that being their name for a stretch of mountains?"

"It is," Vail said. "When you get around to looking it up on your map, you'll find that the Sierra Madre Oriental starts up north of Monterrey and sort of curves east just about all the way down south to Mexico City."

"Sure, I remember now," Longarm said. "And I guess you'll recall a case I worked a while back, the time that outlaw Clell Miller busted away from our boys in El

Paso?" When Vail nodded, he went on. "I had to chase Miller over a lot of country on the other side of the Rio Grande, almost down to where them mountains we're talking about get started."

"Then you won't be a stranger to where this case is likely to take you," Vail suggested.

"Not perzactly a stranger, but I don't know the country all that well, Billy."

"Then you'll have a chance to get acquainted with it again," Vail said. "Now, to get around all the red tape that these orders from Washington are wrapped up in, you're after a fellow that's—well, I guess you'd call him a sort of yard boss in this gold-stealing. His name's Carlos O'Riley, and—"

"Whoa, Billy! Pull up on the reins!" Longarm broke in. "Was I hearing you right? You did say Carlos O'Riley, didn't you?" When Vail nodded, Longarm asked him, "Which is this fellow, Mexican or Irish?"

"What it says in the orders from Washington is that he's the son of an Irishman who came to Mexico with the old San Patricio Brigade."

"That just tells me a lot more about nothing," Longarm protested.

"Then you've never heard of the San Patricio Brigade?" Vail asked.

"If I've heard about it, I just plain disremember now, Billy. But the way you popped right out with it, I sorta got the idea you know it pretty well. Suppose you tell me about it."

"Why, the San Patricio Brigade goes back quite a way, to when the Mexicans were having one of their revolutions. It seems to me that it was the second one, or maybe the third. Anyhow, it was one of the times when the old Mexican families were trying to get rid of

41

one of their bosses. I can't recall whether it was Juarez or Diaz, but I guess it must've been Diaz."

"And never got much of anyplace, as I recall. But if I ain't wrong, they had a few tries at most of 'em, Billy," Longarm said when Vail fell into a moment of silent thought.

"Whichever time it was, they were having a revolution," Vail went on. "And as I remember it, a bunch of Irishmen back in the old country got the idea of mixing in with it to help the common people, so they got together what they called the San Patricio Brigade."

"And come over to Mexico to help what turned out to be the losing side," Longarm added when Vail paused for breath.

"Exactly," the chief marshal said. "Except that the fighting had already stopped before they got here. Most of the San Patricio bunch just turned around and went back home, but some stayed in Mexico and a few of them married local girls."

"I take it this Carlos O'Riley is one that stayed?"

"Both him and his father," Vail replied. "And from what I recall running across in all that mess of papers I got from Washington, the old boy's still alive somewhere in Mexico. Not that it matters a whole lot. Even if the old man's still around he'd be too feeble to do much. It's his son who's mixed up in this gold-stealing."

"Then going by what you said, I'm likely to have a mite of trouble, if the boy likes to fight like his daddy."

"Let's just say he won't be putting out a welcome mat when he finds out what you're there for," Vail said. "Because that family's one of the richest in Mexico."

"And this young Carlos fellow?" Longarm asked. "He's got a hand in this case I'm going to be working?"

"Of course he has, or I never would've mentioned him. He's the one that's muddied up the water. Him and a few like him."

"Billy, all you're doing now is getting me more mixed up about this case," Longarm said, shaking his head. "Maybe you better go over it one step at a time. Start from the beginning or from the back end, whichever suits you better. Who in hell is it I'm after, and what did they do to get us after 'em?"

"It'd take the day and part of the night to tell you all the ins and outs of this case, Long," Vail said. "You'll see all that when you go over the case papers. But maybe if I hit a few of the high spots again it'd clear things up a bit."

"I'd be mighty obliged if you did just that."

"It's a little bit hard to know where to start," Vail said. "And if I had my say, this case ought to be worked by the Secret Service. But to boil it down as near as I can to bare bones, our government's been buying a lot of gold from Mexico these last few years. It still is, for that matter, because of the boom the country's in right now. We need that Mexican gold to back up our paper money the way the law says we've got to."

"All right, Billy, I understand about that," Longarm said when Vail did not go on. "But what's it got to do with this case?"

"Well, for the most part the gold we buy from Mexico is coins they mint down below the border. They won't sell ingots, just coined money. Anyhow, a while back—nobody's sure just when—a lot of those Mexican coins started turning out to be nothing but brass plated with gold."

"Which means the Treasury's being robbed," Longarm said. "And anybody with half an eye open can see when that happens it means everybody in the country gets taken for part of what's stolen, Billy, even me and you."

"Exactly," Vail said. "And the Secret Service won't work the case because it's part of the Treasury Department."

"Now, that don't make good sense," Longarm said with a frown. "Not unless . . ."

"Unless they're afraid some of their own agents might be tied into it," Vail finished. "I don't suppose it takes much figuring for you to see that the big high muckety-mucks back in Washington are shying away from having the Secret Service investigate its own people. That's why we got handed the job."

"Now it's all starting to make some sense," Longarm said. "Except that I'd like for you to tell me why I'm winding up with this damn mixed-up case in my lap."

"Because the Attorney General himself asked me to put you on it," Vail replied. "Not that I wouldn't have done just that myself if he hadn't. And you'll see the whole thing's pretty clear after you've read through all this paperwork I got from Washington."

"Which I don't aim to do right this minute," Longarm told him. "If I'm going down to Mexico, I'll need to take care of a few chores before I start. For one thing, I'll want to get my guns looked at, and there's a rough place inside of my left boot that needs tending to. On top of that, there's a few other little jobs, like closing the file on Blaze Brady."

"Well, I'm not saying you've got to start tomorrow," Vail told him. "But you know how it is with the brass back East. Do what you need to, but don't take too long. The sooner . . ."

"The better," Longarm finished. "Sure. Well, give me a day or two here in Denver, Billy. Enough time to get my little chores done and sleep a night or two without having to keep one eye open to be on watch for some damn outlaw sneaking up on me. Then I'll head for Mexico and see what kind of a job I'm going to run into this time."

Longarm stepped outside the doorway of the Hotel del Norte in Monterrey, where he'd just registered, and stopped to light a fresh cigar. For a moment he stood gazing along the street in front of him, glad to be standing up. His knees still twitched occasionally after the long trip cramped in one of the hard bumpy seats of the Ferrocariles de Mexico railroad coach.

Daylight was making its last stand. In a few of the small shops lining the street lights were glowing, but the doors of most of them still stood open. There were few people moving along the street in either direction, and after a quick glance he decided that the hour was too late for those having business to take care of and too early for those out to enjoy an evening on the town.

"It's been such a long time since you was here that you've forgot that folks down here in Mexico don't do things the way you're used to, old son," he told himself out loud. "Now, let's see. That place run by a fellow named Benito, where you finally found some Tom Moore the last time you come here on a case, wasn't too far away from the hotel. All you got to do is figure out which way you turned."

Turning to the right on impulse, Longarm walked slowly to the street corner, his boot heels crunching on the crumbling bricks of the narrow sidewalk. A glance in each direction along the intersecting street told him that his choice had not been a good one.

Retracing his steps, he passed the hotel and went on to the opposite corner. At his first glance along

the intersecting street he saw a sign which he remembered, and wasted no time covering the short remaining
distance to the *cantina* he had in mind. The evening was
too early for the place to be crowded. Longarm saw only
four men in the place when he entered, and one of them
was the barkeep, busy with the job of arranging bottles
and glasses on the back-bar shelves.

As he walked up to the bar he slid a silver dollar out of
his pocket and dropped it on the surface. The barkeep did
not stop work with the sound, but glanced quickly over his
shoulder and went on with his job as he said, *"Momento,
señor. Tan pronto como . . ."* As he spoke the man behind
the bar glanced in the mirror. His face lighted into a
smile and he raised his voice. "Brazolargo! *Amigo!"*

Setting the glasses he was holding on the narrow back
bar, he turned and stepped up to stand opposite Longarm.
"De seguro, eet ees you! *Bienvenido, compadre!"*

While he and the barkeep shook hands, Longarm said,
"It's me, all right, Nito. I promised you I'd be sure to
drop in was I ever back this way, and here I am"

"E-stay where you are," the barman said. "I know
what eet ees you weesh."

Turning away from Longarm, the barkeep hurried
to the end of the back bar and opened the door of a
cabinet at its base. He reached inside and took out a
bottle, picked up a shot glass on his way back to where
Longarm stood waiting, and set the bottle and glass on
the bar in front of him.

Longarm smiled when he saw Tom Moore's familiar
name on the bottle's dusty label. He said, "You mean
you been saving this since I was here the last time?"

"De seguro," Benito said. "Eet ees not easy to buy
such wheesky een Mexico. You are e-say you weel come
back, after you have done so moch for me wheen you are

46

here before, so I put eet away. Now you are here. I have eet for you."

"Well, I got to give you credit for being a man of your word, Nito," Longarm said.

He pulled the cork from the bottle, filled the glass which Benito had placed on the bar, and lifted it in salute to the barkeep before tossing off the big swallow of pungent whiskey. As he slipped a fresh cigar from his pocket and lighted it, the barman refilled the shot glass.

"E-tell me," Benito said as he pushed the glass closer to Longarm. "You are e-come to find more of *los ladrones* who are run to our country to hide from your law?"

Longarm had learned to trust the saloon-keeper's discretion during their earlier encounter. He did not hesitate, but nodded in response to Benito's question.

"That's about the size of it," he replied. "But from what little I know so far, the kind of crooks I'm trying to run down on this trip ain't the same breed as the little scallywags that was giving you such a lot of trouble when I was here before."

"How ees thees?" Benito asked as a frown crept over his face. "*Ladrón* ees *ladrón,* no?"

Longarm took another puff of his cigar as he silently debated the wisdom of discussing the details of his present case with the bar owner. Then he decided that Benito must certainly be as reliable as—and perhaps more reliable than—the notoriously untrustworthy Mexican lawmen whom he'd be forced to consult if he followed the instructions from Washington that Billy Vail had given him.

"Sure," Longarm replied. "Crooks just go right on being crooks, even when they try to hide behind a lawman's badge."

"Eef you are e-say that our *rurales* and our Policía Central do not honor the badges they wear, you are

47

e-speak true," Benito said. "We, *la gente,* know thees well. And they are not alone. From our Presidente on down, they are e-steal. They are e-steal from us, *la gente,* they are e-steal from each other. And they are e-steal from your country too. They sell you brass and not the gold you pay them for."

Longarm had downed a sip of Tom Moore while Benito was speaking. For a moment the significance of what the barman had said did not sink home. He waited until the last drops of rye had trickled down his throat before he said, "You mind telling me what you mean by that, Nito?"

Benito glanced at the three men who were drinking at the end of the bar. He shook his head, hesitated for a moment, then drew his hand across his throat. Dropping his voice to a whisper, he said, "I am not baby who came yesterday from hees mother's belly, Brazolargo. Eef I am to tell you all I know and *los rurales* learn of eet, I am dead man."

Longarm was silent for a moment. He'd worked enough cases in Mexico to know that the country had its full share of thieves who were also merciless killers.

Following Benito's example, he kept his voice low as he said, "I know this ain't the place or the time to be talking, Nito. And you don't owe me nothing either. But if you'd maybe feel like telling me anything that'd help me close my case down here, I'd be mighty much obliged."

"Of thees I must theenk," the barkeeper said.

"Sure," Longarm told him. Then he dropped his voice. "Now, if you want to, you can come up to my room in the hotel when you close up, and we'll have a little confab. I'm in Room 210, and I'll leave the door unlocked. You just do what you feel like doing."

Before Benito could reply, Longarm dropped a half eagle on the bar and walked out of the saloon.

Chapter 5

Longarm was lying full-length on the bed in his hotel room, watching the smoke from his cigar as it shimmered upward through the lamplight in lazy gray streams. He'd just taken off his boots after draping his coat and vest on the bedpost and hanging his gunbelt over them, making sure that the butt of the holstered revolver would be within easy reach after he'd stretched out. Now he was waiting and wondering if Benito was going to accept the invitation to join him.

Soon he'd puffed his cigar down to an inch-long butt, and was reaching for the saucer on the lamp stand that served the room as an ashtray. Longarm was almost ready to believe that Benito had decided not to pay him a visit when a light tapping on the door broke the late night silence. Though he knew the knock almost certainly announced Benito's promised visit, Longarm had learned long ago that outlaws had long memories and carried grudges against lawmen who might have crossed their crooked paths. He'd escaped more than once by narrow margins from felons seeking revenge, and took no chances.

Sliding his Colt from its holster as he rose, Longarm crossed the room to answer the knock. As he'd guessed, Benito was standing in the hallway. Stepping back, Longarm motioned for the tavern-owner to enter.

"I have regret so late to be," Benito said. "But after you are go, ees many customers come een."

"Now, I ain't one to blame a man that tends to his own business first," Longarm replied, turning to face tavern-owner after holstering his Colt. "If a man didn't pay any mind to where his bread and butter's coming from, I'd mark him down in my book for being a fool. And I thank you for coming up here to help me out with this case I'm on after you've just put a long day's work behind you."

"Maybe so to you thees ees just what you call a case," Benito said. A frown twitched his face. "But to me eet ees much more."

Longarm shook his head. "I reckon I don't perzactly follow you."

"Eet ees because our *familia* long ago have make *juramento fealidad* to our martyred leader Maximiliano." Benito saw the faint frown that rippled over Longarm's face. "Thees ees mean we—"

Longarm broke in. "Hold on, Nito. I'm figuring out what you said. Leastwise I think I am. And I got to brush up on your lingo, because I ain't had no reason to talk it for a while and I'm bound to need it in some pinch or other. Now, if I ain't forgotten too much of what little I know, your folks put their heads together and decided they'd just keep on doing what they figured Maximilian

50

would want them to. It's like something you'd sworn to on the Bible, ain't it?"

"De seguro," Benito agreed.

"So you'd do whatever your kin did, even if you weren't around when they were fighting on his side." Benito acknowledged Longarm's interpretation with a nod. Longarm went on. "That was quite a while back, and things got a way of changing. If I recall correctly, ain't your man Maximilian been dead for a pretty good spell?"

"En verdad," Benito said. "But weeth our people thees things we are not forget. My father and hees father before him fought beside Maximiliano to free our people and when they rise again, I weel fight as they did."

"You mean you got another revolution puffing up right now?" Longarm asked.

"You make the good guess, *amigo*," Benito said, his voice very sober. "And what I have tell you ees true. The gold our enemies rob from your country ees for buy guns and pay soldiers. They know that eef they do not have more e-strength they weel be beaten when we of the people rise."

"When we was talking in your place a little while back, you dropped a sorta hint about gold-stealing," Longarm said. He'd taken out a cigar while he was speaking. Now he flicked his thumbnail over a match and began puffing the long thin cheroot to light it.

"Do I make meestake wheen I theenk you are come here to e-stop thees?" Benito asked.

Longarm waited until his cigar was drawing properly before he replied. Realizing that he'd need more information from Benito, he decided that he must take the saloon-keeper at least partly into his confidence. He said, "Now, you're bound to know I can't give you

51

a straight-out yes-or-no answer to a question like that, Nito. Let's just say that I was sent to find out if there is some crookedness."

"Thees e-stealing you are learn about, ees eet to e-stamp round pieces from brass and theen put coat of gold on theem so they look to be *moneda acuñada* the U.S.?" Benito ventured.

Frowning as he replied, Longarm said, "It seems to me like you know more about this case I'm on than I do myself."

"Wheen men at *cantina* dreenk *aguardiente* and *tequila* they talk as they weel not do een other places," Benito said. "All I am do ees leesten."

"From the way you just been talking, I'd say you do a pretty good job of it too. Is listening to your customers how you found out about them cheating on the gold pieces they sell to the United States Treasury in Washington?"

"*Verdaderamente,*" Benito said.

"I guess you'd know pretty well who these fellows are?"

"There are in my customers only a few of those who make the coins een the *casa de moneda.*" Benito shrugged. "They are workers only, *peones*. The *ricos* who take the *dinero fraudulento* and use eet to cheat your country are men of importance and power, high in the *gobierno.*"

Now Longarm was beginning to put together the somewhat cryptic reports he'd been given by Billy Vail, and could get a clearer picture of the job he'd been sent to do. He was silent for a moment, then asked Benito, "Do you happen to know anything about a man named Carlos O'Riley?"

"I do not e-say that I know heem, Longarm. He does

not come to dreenk een such leetle place like I have. But ees name everybody know in Monterrey. He ees from one of the old *rico* families."

Longarm kept his voice casual as he said, "This O'Riley fellow is just part of what I got to ask you about, Nito. What I'd sure like for you to do is tell me some more about the fellow, even if you don't know him man-to-man."

"He ees *rico,* I am *peon.*" Benito shrugged. "You have learn of Mexico enough to know he would not weeth me be *compañero.* I tell you only what I hear."

"Well, what've you heard about him then?"

Benito sat frowning silently for a moment. "No more as I am know of others like heem. Of gossip, I hear much. He ees *hacendado,* thees O'Riley, ees live on beeg *rancho,* et ees near to Las Cumbres, these are hills north from town, along the Sierra Oriental. He ees have many head of cattle, has bank here, has beautiful wife, no *niños.*"

"You said something about gossip."

"Ees always gossip, *amigo.*" Benito smiled. "And only some ees true. I am hear that Don Carlos ees have many women here and een other places. I am hear that he ees want to be more beeg man as now. *Ademas,* I am hear that he ees *compañero* of el Presidente and I have hear that he ees no more *compañero* of el Presidente."

"And which do you believe?"

Benito shrugged. "Ees both maybe true."

"What sorta stumps me right now is that I ain't got much to go on about where to start looking for them cheating scallywags." Longarm smiled ruefully. "But if this O'Riley's a friend of the President, and he's got a bank, he'd sure be about the likeliest man I could put a name to right now for being mixed up in this gold swindle. My job's to prove it's going on and figure out a way to stop it."

"Weeth thees I can geeve only small help," Benito said. "Maybe so eef I leesten weeth more care to talk een *cantina*, I am hear more."

"Well, you already helped me a lot more'n I got any right to expect," Longarm assured him. "But if you hear any more little bits and pieces, I'd sure thank you for passing 'em on."

"*De seguro*," Benito promised. He stood up. "Ees no more I can theenk of to tell you, *amigo*. Eef I do hear sometheeng—"

Longarm broke in. "Just keep it under your hat till I stop by your place next time. It's been a while since I was here last, so I'll need to poke around and get acquainted again, maybe ask a question here and there. But I'll stop in at your place pretty regular, Nito. Now, I know you've had a real long day, and so have I. We both need some sleep."

Both men stood up. Benito started for the door, turned as he reached it to wave good-bye, and closed it behind him. Longarm stepped across the room to lock it. He shed his shirt as he walked back to the bed, sat down long enough to peel off his socks and trousers, then stretched out luxuriously. Within two minutes he was asleep.

A persistent ray of sunshine dancing across his face from the edge of the window shade brought Longarm fully awake. He sat up in bed, his hand going by long habit to the butt of his Colt. By the time he'd reached up to the head of the bedstead where the revolver hung suspended by the gunbelt and closed his hand on its grip, he'd been awake long enough to realize that hunger rather than danger had awakened him.

"Old son," he muttered in the stillness of the hotel room as he released the Colt and twisted to sit on the bedside, "what's wrong is that you got a bad case of the hungries. And there ain't nobody going to bring your breakfast in, so it's up to you to get up and go after it."

A half hour later, sponge-bathed and shaved, his saddlebags and rifle lying on the floor beside him, Longarm was sitting at a table in the hotel's small restaurant just off the lobby. In front of him, a platter containing a thick slab of of dark red ham the size of his hand, flanked by a pair of frizzle-edged fried eggs, was getting his full attention.

Having breakfasted in the past at similar hotels in Mexico, Longarm had not been surprised by the generous portion, and wasted no time dealing with his morning repast. Using his clasp-knife after trying out the dull case-knife of the table setting, he cut a bite-sized chunk of ham and began chewing it vigorously while trying to slice a bite off the almost stone-hard fried eggs.

Longarm had worked his way through almost half of the generous servings when a small stirring at the door leading to the lobby drew his attention. He glanced toward the door. Though the two men talking in low voices with the restaurant's lone waiter wore no badges nor insignia of rank, Longarm had seen their like before. He would have had to be blind not to have recognized them as *rurales* by their oversized sombreros and the ornate gold and silver braid that almost hid the fabric of both their hats and their waist-length *charro* jackets.

Being careful to give no indication that he'd even noticed them, Longarm cut himself another bite of ham while he covertly flicked his eyes toward the new arrivals. He'd noticed when entering the restaurant that it had neither windows nor a door other than the one by which he'd entered.

Now he quickly swept the room's walls with flicks of his eyes. The brief inspection confirmed his earlier casual observation that the door by which he'd entered was the only way out. There was no way for him to avoid the *rurales* except by leaping up and trying to burst between them.

Even though his instincts had started warning bells ringing in his mind when the *rurales* arrived, Longarm carefully ignored them. The bite of ham that he'd cut was still impaled on his fork, and he lifted it to his mouth and started chewing. Before he'd lowered his hand holding the fork to rest on the edge of the table, the pair of *rurales* had started toward him. He continued to ignore them except for occasional sidewise glimpses, and kept chewing his morsel of ham as they threaded their way through the tables.

Longarm was still chewing when the *rurales* stopped beside his table, shifting their positions slightly in order to flank his chair. Longarm looked up and nodded, then gestured toward his moving jaws. The *rurales* ignored his gesture, their eyes now fixed on his face.

"You are the man call Custis Long, no?" one of them asked. His English was only slightly accented. "The one who is claim to be of the United States police?"

"Well, my name's Custis Long, all right," Longarm replied after he'd swallowed his bite of ham. "I don't reckon you'd come beelining over here without knowing that. And I don't claim to be nothing that I ain't. Not any more'n I'd try to hide what I am. I'm a United States marshal, and I got the badge and the papers that'll prove it."

"Theen you will show me these papers," one of the men said. He made no effort to disguise his hostility; it was expressed in both his face and in the tone of his voice.

For a fleeting moment Longarm's mind was busy juggling his options. He knew that he'd be at a disadvantage if he started a fight in the cramped and crowded space of the restaurant, and knew equally well the trigger-happy habits of the *rurales*. He took the course that seemed to suit the moment best. Bending forward to reach his saddlebags on the floor beside him, Longarm had just slipped his hand into the side pocket of the saddlebag holding his papers when a jarring blow from the pistol butt of one of the *rurales* crashed down on his head and he lurched to the floor unconscious.

Longarm's first blurred impression of his surroundings when consciousness returned was that he was surrounded by an all-prevalent and highly offensive odor. He shook his head to clear his mind and started to lift his hand to his throbbingly aching head, but the movement of his arms was stopped almost at once with a metallic clinking and a painful biting of cold steel on his wrists.

His eyes had opened only to slits when Longarm first began shaking his head, but now the fuzziness of his vision was beginning to clear. As he blinked his eyelids wider apart Longarm could see that he was in a small room. Twisting his head, he saw the door behind him was opened a handsbreadth, and also saw that the room had a single high barred window, closed with wooden shutters outside the bars.

The only light seeped through the partly opened door and the thin cracks in the shutters, but even that small amount of illumination allowed him to get a good idea of his surroundings. The room was barren of furniture except for two or three chairs like the one in which he was sitting, his wrists clamped into shackles anchored by chains to its arms, and a small table against the wall. Longarm could see his Colt on the table and his saddlebags on the floor beside it.

Now Longarm tested his feet to see if they'd also been chained in place. He found that he could move his legs freely, and tried to stand up, but the arm shackles bound him so closely to the chair that its weight pushing the edge of the seat against his knees kept him from straightening his legs. He relaxed and settled back into the seat of the chair. His movements caused the chains to begin tinkling and a man's voice rose from somewhere beyond the partly opened door.

"Attenderse! El gringo despertamiento!"

"Pues, nos asuntonos," a second man replied.

Now Longarm twisted his head to determine the source of the voices. His movement might well have been a signal, for almost immediately the thunking of booted feet sounded. In a moment two men came through the door. They left it open, and the light in the room brightened enough to give Longarm a good look at his jailers.

Though the men did not look alike, they'd been cast from much the same mold. The taller of the pair had a high-arched hawklike nose so long that it appeared to bisect his upper lip. Its thin nostrils kept expanding and contracting as though they were controlled by some sort of clockwork mechanism. His protruding chin tapered to a point and his nostrils were high-arched, wide, and flaring.

His companion was a short man, his head barely rising to the level of the other *rurale*'s shoulders. His skin was of a darker hue. His cheekbones bulged and seemed to compress his features. His nose was a round snub that appeared to merge with his broad chubby-cheeked face, his chin a rounded puff below thick bulging lips that were almost completely hidden by a sweeping ink-black mustache.

Longarm did not remember having seen either of the men before, but their uniforms were the same as those which had been worn by the *rurales* who'd arrested him. He said, "I still don't know why them two men of yours grabbed onto me and brought me here. And I don't know why you bundled me up like a bale of hay this way. What'll I have to do to find out?"

"Facilidad," the chubby *rurale* replied. Then he realized that he'd replied in Spanish. "Ees easy. You are to tell us why you have to Mexico come, and who ees send you here."

"Well, I sure ain't broke no laws I'd know about," Longarm replied. "And I just come here to look at the scenery if that's what's bothering you."

"Eef thees ees true, theen how are you to esplain the papers you are carry een your saddlebag?" the rotund *rurale* asked. "Why are you een Estados Unidos care from what we are do een Mexico?"

"Why, all that's just some working papers that I forgot to take outa my saddlebags before I started here," Longarm replied. He had little hope that his bluff would work, for the *rurale* who was questioning him seemed to have a reasonably good understanding of English and had almost certainly gone through his papers and examined everything they contained.

"You are lie to me first, now you are lie again!" the *rurale* exclaimed. "Do you theenk I cannot read theem?"

"Well, you ain't done nothing yet to prove what you've

said about reading that batch of old papers. If you did, you sure ain't read 'em rightly, or I wouldn't be all chained up in this chair," Longarm told him. Knowing that his best and perhaps only chance to regain his freedom was to bluff his way out, he went on. "Now, the way you're doing things, I got an idea you might be bluffing yourself."

"Es mentiroso!" the *rurale* blustered. His face was flushed with anger now.

"Well, now," Longarm replied, his voice level and cool. "If you think I'm lying to you, just go ahead and prove it."

The *rurale* exploded. "Do not forget, you are *prisionero*! You are to answer me wheen I ask the question!"

"Now, I don't know about any law saying I got to do that," Longarm replied. His voice was level, his tone one of a man trying to reason with a small boy who was misbehaving.

"Hah!" the *rurale* snorted. "We weel see how long you are e-keep the *silencio* wheen you e-shake hands weeth the leetle glove we keep for the stubborn ones e-like you!" Turning to the other *rurale,* who had stood watching in silence, he said, "Ramon! *Llevarse la manopla!*"

Chapter 6

Longarm tried to suppress a puzzled frown when he heard the man's command and saw the other *rurale* leave the room. He tried to translate the last few words spoken by the *rurale*, but they were not included in his somewhat limited knowledge of Border Spanish. He was still trying to figure out what the pair intended to do to him when Ramon, the tall thin *rurale,* returned carrying a short thick slab of wood which had straps dangling from its sides and an arm or lever of some sort sticking out of one end.

Longarm only glanced at these minor details. His attention was concentrated on the silvery-looking glove that spanned the top of the wooden block. The glove was now close enough for him to see clearly. He stared at it, then realized that it was not a glove but an ancient gauntlet made of skillfully jointed steel strips, and that quite probably it had been fabricated in the days when fighting men went to battle wearing armor.

"Conoces que tengo aquí?" the man standing in front of Longarm asked.

As he spoke, he gestured toward the contrivance his companion had brought in. Although Longarm's knowledge of Spanish was enough for him to understand the question, he ignored it. His mind was concentrated on trying to puzzle out the use of the strange device. The *rurale* who'd questioned him waited for a moment, then shrugged and turned to Ramon.

"Ponete en puesto," he ordered.

"Sí, Luis," Ramon said.

Ramon strapped the heavy wooden base to the chair's arm. Then he fumbled a key out of his pocket. Longarm's unasked questions were answered when Ramon grasped his right forearm in a firm grip and unlocked the handcuff on its wrist.

"Quieres ayuda, Ramon?" Luis asked.

"No es necesario," Ramon replied.

When Ramon removed the shackles Longarm tried to twist his arm out of the *rurale's* grasp, and now the man called Ramon jerked his head toward Luis, who stepped up and added his strength to that of his companion. Their combined strength was greater than Longarm's, and he had no choice but to allow them to slide his right hand into the metal gauntlet.

Longarm was well aware that in the flurry of their struggles the *rurales* had overlooked returning the shackles to his left hand. He let it fall unobtrusively into his lap, and sat motionless while the *rurales* strapped his right arm to the wooden slab supporting the gauntlet. Their job completed, Ramon stood up and gestured toward the chair arm.

"Es acobado," he said. *"Cual destaho quieres?"*

"Comienzamos," Luis replied. *"Yo acabare."*

With a nod, Ramon grasped the lever that rose from the gauntlet's base and began to push it forward. Longarm clamped his jaws tightly as he felt the gauntlet begin to compress his imprisoned hand. Though the pressure was gentle at that moment, he knew that it would be increased and that he must move both swiftly and cautiously.

A quick glance told Longarm that both *rurales* were absorbed in watching the steel gauntlet as its pressure continued to tighten on his hand. The pain that was beginning to cramp his wrist and fingers told him the rest of the story—that only the speediest possible action would save him from what would quickly become a crippling torture.

Very slowly but quite steadily, keeping his eyes on the two *rurales*, Longarm began raising his left arm from his lap. He moved it slowly until it was high enough to allow him to slide his fingers behind his belt buckle. Watching the two *rurales* closely, Longarm groped for the little double-barreled derringer that was concealed there.

At last he got his fingers on the derringer's butt. He began working, guided by the pressure on his fingertips, inching the stubby little weapon out of its soft leather case, keeping his his eyes on Ramon and Luis without moving his head.

Longarm had drawn the derringer often enough in similar tight situations to slide the miniature-sized pistol from its sheath without giving any indication of what he was doing. He closed his fingers over the sloping butt of the little three-inch-long pistol and flicked his eyes from Ramon to Luis to be sure that the attention of both men was still absorbed in watching the gauntlet tighten.

In the few minutes required for Longarm to complete his maneuver the sharp edges of the steel glove's metal strips had grown from an annoying pressure to one that was steadily becoming more painful. Longarm now had the derringer firmly in his hand, his trigger finger in place. He slid his arm upward, keeping his eyes fixed on the *rurales*. Neither of them had taken their eyes off the gauntlet, which was now biting sharply into Longarm's imprisoned hand.

At the range of only a foot or two, Longarm did not need to take careful aim. He brought up the derringer, and with its muzzle only inches from Ramon's face triggered off one of his two shots. At the instant when the red spurt of muzzle blast was still brightening the gloom of the dimly lighted room Longarm was twisting his hand to bring the derringer to bear on Luis.

His second shot sounded before the echoes of the first had died away. Ramon was still crumpling to the floor, but had not yet landed outstretched when Luis sagged into a motionless sprawl and joined him as a second huddled corpse. Longarm waited for a moment, listening to make sure that the shots had not alerted other *rurales* who might be in the building, but heard no shouts, no pounding footsteps.

"Looks like your luck's good right now, old son," Longarm muttered under his breath. "And you better be careful to keep it going that way."

Letting the derringer drop to the floor, Longarm twisted in the uncomfortable chair until he could reach the lever that controlled the biting pressure of the steel gauntlet. It yielded easily as he reversed its angle, and Longarm loosed a long breath of relief when the pains that had been shooting through his hand ebbed away. Then he carefully withdrew his imprisoned right hand from the gauntlet.

Longarm glanced at his hand. Its back was lightly scored with a series of parallel red weals where the edges of the glove's metal strips had begun to bite in. A few small drops of blood were beginning to ooze from some of the red lines where the edges of the gauntlet's steel had bitten the deepest, but when Longarm flexed his hand he felt very little pain.

"Well, old son," Longarm said aloud, "you got off a lot lighter'n it looked like you was going to. Now, you better gather up what truck you got here and make tracks as fast as you can. For all you know, there's more *rurales* somewheres in this place, and even if that derringer ain't loud as a six-gun, shots got a way of carrying."

Moving as silently and swiftly as he could, Longarm picked up his Colt and restored it to his holster before looking through the door into the *rurales'* office to make sure it was empty. Then he took the few minutes required to dig two fresh cartridges out of his necessary bag, reload the derringer, and replace it in its concealed holster.

When he'd finished his quickly handled chores, Longarm stood silently for a moment, holding his rifle, listening for sounds which might indicate that other *rurales* in the building might be coming to investigate the shots he'd fired. He heard no sounds indicating that danger. He stepped into the office and saw two doors, one of which led to the rest of the building. It had a bolt instead of a lock, and he threw it, hoping to defer discovery of the two bodies on the floor inside the small room.

Picking up his rifle and saddlebags, Longarm stepped to the second door, which led outside. As he cracked it open, a bright line of daylight met his eyes. He blinked at the unaccustomed brightness of high noon and for the first time was aware of how long he'd been in the torture chamber of the *rurales*.

For a moment he stood motionless, letting his eyes adjust to the outside glare. Then he slipped through the door and closed it carefully. Carrying his saddlebags in his left hand and his rifle in his right, never looking back, and always keeping his ears cocked for the shouts which would warn him of pursuers, Longarm walked with long steps in the direction of the hotel.

Although the sun was at or near its zenith, the streets of Monterrey were almost deserted. The few pedestrians who were abroad paid no attention to Longarm as he walked steadily ahead. He reached the bulk of the hotel building and turned into the street that ran behind it. As he'd hoped, the door of Benito's tavern stood ajar. Slipping through the door, he saw Benito busy wiping glasses at the back bar.

"Morning, Nito," Longarm said as the barkeeper turned away from his job. "Or afternoon, whichever it is. I ain't had time to figure it out yet."

"Ees right from *la medio día,*" Benito said. "But ees not like you that you do not know such theengs. Are you have the trouble, Longarm?"

"A mite, but nothing I couldn't get out of," Longarm replied. "Except that I wouldn't like to run into any of your *rurales* right this minute."

"They are e-look for you?" Benito asked.

"If they ain't looking for me now, they will be pretty soon. I figure I better cut a shuck getting out of town, but I need to find out about this Carlos O'Riley fellow first. You got any ideas about where he might be?"

"He ees have bank, and ees maybe there," Benito said. "Or maybe so he ees go to hees *rancho.* Ees een Las Cumbres, *al norte.*"

"Sure, I recollect you told me about it, except you didn't say how far it'd be from here."

66

"Ees one day ride, but long day. Ees not but one road, you could not mees eet."

"And I reckon his bank'd be someplace pretty near here?"

"Ees past hotel leetle way, on same e-street," Benito told him. "You weel find eet easy. Ees have beeg sign on top. Banco Central."

"Then I oughta be able to get there without too much trouble. Now, I got one favor to ask you, Nito. If I don't show up back here inside of a week, let's say, you send a wire to my chief in Denver."

"De seguro," Benito replied. "How I am to know who ees to get thees wire?"

"Just send it to Chief Marshal Vail at the U.S. marshal's office in Denver, Colorado. All you got to say in it is that I've run into some trouble. Billy'll know what to do when he gets it."

"Bueno," Benito said. "But *hace cuidado,* Longarm. He ees e-smart man and mean one, thees Don Carlos O'Riley."

"Oh, I'll keep my eyes peeled," Longarm promised. "And now I better get myself moving before I get myself into another jackpot like I was just now."

Leaving Benito's saloon, Longarm stopped at the hotel only long enough to settle his bill and reclaim his livery horse. He reined it into the main street and turned in the direction Benito had given him. The last case which had brought Longarm to Monterrey was far in the past, and when he'd seen the town at that time it had been little more than a sleepy village.

Now its streets were lined with stores, even though many of them were small and housed in buildings that were often no wider than a man's outstretched arms. More than half the new structures were built of bricks—

not adobe bricks, but the shining modern kiln-made variety. Though the rutted thoroughfare was not crowded, there was now a fair number of pedestrians as well as a few buggies and wagons.

Letting his horse pick its own way along the street, Longarm kept scanning the store fronts, looking for the sign he'd been told would identify the bank. He saw it at last. In fact, he could not have missed seeing it even if he'd been blindfolded.

The bank occupied a building that was obviously new and took up the frontage of half a city block. It was constructed of glistening glazed orange-hued bricks that sparkled in contrast to the older adobe-brick buildings flanking it. The sign that rose above its imposing facade bore foot-high letters, black on a crimson background, identifying it as Banco Central.

"Now that's a place a man sure can't miss, old son," Longarm said under his breath as he fished one of his long slim cigars from his vest pocket and lighted it. "Why, for purty it could give that new Windsor Hotel in Denver cards and spades and still take high-low jack and game. Looks like this Don Carlos O'Riley's either a rich man right now, or he's figuring on getting rich in a hurry."

For another moment or two he stayed in his saddle, studying the building. Then he dismounted and looped the reins of his horse around the hitch rail that spanned the building's front. A couple of long strides took him to the door. When Longarm stepped inside the bank and stopped a few steps beyond the door, the same newness met his eyes everywhere he looked.

Three or four men sat at desks behind a waist-high marble partition. There were others standing behind the tellers' windows, but regardless of their positions they wore glistening silk jackets of a conservative light-brown shade. Though a few of them had cultivated mustaches, the majority were clean-shaven, and their neatly combed black hair shone with pomade.

Before Longarm could flick his eyes around the entire perimeter of the spacious interior a man at one of the desks rose and stepped up to him. "Do you perhaps need assistance, *señor?*" he asked. "I can see that you are strange to our bank here."

"I'm looking for your boss man, Don Carlos O'Riley," Longarm replied.

"Regretfully, Don Carlos is not here."

"Maybe you can tell me when he will be?" Longarm asked.

"This I am afraid I cannot do," the man replied. "He has gone to his *rancho*. It is some distance from here. He did not inform us when he will return. But if you have business here with the bank, I will be glad to give you any help that you might require."

Longarm shook his head. "It's him I got to talk to. This ranch he's at, would that be up north a ways? Up by a stand of little mountains called Las Cumbres that shows on my map?"

For a moment the man did not reply. Then he nodded a bit reluctantly. "I can see that you are acquainted with Don Carlos's habits, *señor*. It will certainly do no harm for me to tell you that you are correct."

"Then maybe I better go on up there and see him," Longarm said. "I'm in a sorta hurry, and ain't really got the time to lallygag around waiting for him to get back."

"I would be most happy to send Don Carlos a message on your behalf," the bank clerk offered.

Longarm shook his head. "What I got to talk about with your boss ain't got a thing to do with the bank,

69

except maybe in a sort of roundabout way. But I'd be mighty obliged if you'd tell me exactly how to get to his ranch."

"There is but the one road for you to take. It is the one that passes the ore smelter on the north of the town. Where Las Cumbres begin to rise there is a smaller road branching from the main one. You will take the right-hand road then. It reaches to Don Carlos's *hacienda* a short distance after you have turned off on the fork."

"I reckon that's all the directions I need," Longarm said. "So I'll be on my way, and I thank you for your help."

For the better part of the dwindling day Longarm had been following the well-beaten path, more trail than road, toward the distant vista of jagged low-rising hills. In the west the sun was now hanging only a short distance above the horizon, and for as far as he could see there were no houses; only the narrow strip of the beaten trail broke the landscape's monotony.

Longarm's ride had been a lonely one, for he'd passed nobody on the way north. After the straggling outskirts of Monterrey were behind him he'd ridden past a dozen small houses set back from the lazily winding road by strips of cultivated land.

Gradually the dwellings had been spaced further and further apart. At last there were no more cultivated fields, only the straggling pale green shoots of chamisal rising a foot or two above brown barren soil. After Longarm had ridden another mile or so even the chamisal vanished and the smooth gently contoured land was broken by low rock outcrops rising in jagged clusters above the lighter-colored soil.

Now the landscape ahead took on a sharply different look, with white and light tan stretches of barren rock. The grade of the road grew steeper and the mountains ahead of him now looked more imposing, high-rising peaks slowly losing their form as the late afternoon became evening.

Longarm realized that he could not hope to reach his goal before total darkness, and began looking for a sheltered place to make a dry camp overnight. He found one sooner than he'd expected, a strip of low brush just a few dozen feet off the road. Reining his horse toward the stand of bushes, he tethered it and took off its saddle.

After a few moments of stomping the low-growing brush in an area large enough to serve as a bed, Longarm spread his saddle blankets out on the crumbled bushes. He put his saddle on one end of the blankets to serve as a pillow. After pulling his rifle from its saddle scabbard, he laid it along one edge of blanket and took off his gunbelt. He placed that on the side opposite the rifle, then stretched out between them.

"It ain't exactly the kinda bed you'd get in a good hotel, old son," he told himself. "But it'll do for a shakedown."

Though he was speaking aloud into empty air, his voice sounded as loud as a shout in the almost total stillness. Taking a final glance around the deserted landscape, and seeing no lights except those which came from the stars, Longarm stretched out. He propped himself up with an elbow while he fished out one of his long thin cigars and lighted it.

Now the darkness was almost complete, for there was no moon. Gradually, Longarm's eyes adjusted to the darkness. He lay propped up until his cigar had been smoked down. Then he leaned out to push its glowing tip into the dry ground. Now he lay motionless, his head on his saddle. After his busy day, Longarm needed no lullabies. After a few moments he was sleeping soundly.

Longarm's sleep was broken only once. A thudding of hoofbeats from the direction of the trail brought him fully awake. His arm moved as though by instinct to grasp his rifle, and before he was sitting fully erect he had the Winchester ready to shoulder. The star shine had not diminished, but the night was still black and impenetrable.

Longarm sat quietly, holding his Winchester across his chest as he listened to the hoofbeats along the trail only a few dozen feet away. Though he strained to pierce the darkness, the horse and its rider remained invisible.

"Whoever that is knows where he's going and is in a hurry to get there," Longarm said aloud as he listened to the rhythmic thuds. "Was he trying to follow your trail, he wouldn't be riding at all in the dark, let along holding such a fast pace."

After growing louder until they passed him, the thuds of hooves on the hard earth faded quickly. When they died away and the night was again silent, Longarm relaxed. He replaced the rifle in its former position and stretched out to go to sleep once more.

Chapter 7

As the first faint hint of dawn was beginning to brighten
the eastern sky and start the darkness retreating, Longarm
woke up. As always when on the trail, he was alert
the moment his eyes opened. When he heard nothing
except the small sounds made by his horse shifting
its feet restlessly, Longarm slid his Colt out of the
folds he'd made in the blanket to form a pillow and
restored the revolver to its holster. Sitting erect in
his blankets, he slipped a cigar from his pocket and
lighted it. He did not stand up until he'd enjoyed
a half-dozen puffs of his stogie and watched the
bluish-gray smoke trail dissipate in the morning air.

Now Longarm got to his feet and stood stretching for
a moment before he began walking in a small circle,
stamping his boot soles on the coarse ground. After a
few moments the annoying little cramps created by his
night on the hard, unyielding makeshift bed had been
worked out of his leg muscles. Even before the muscles

in his legs no longer complained, his stomach had begun to growl each time he moved.

Going to his saddlebags, Longarm dug out his trail rations, a small neat oilcloth-wrapped packet which contained a sizeable chunk of hard-cured sausage and a generous handful of crumbled soda crackers. He munched at the food while the sky grew steadily lighter. By the time he'd eaten enough to stop his stomach's complaints, Longarm could see the jagged outline of the Cumbres de Monterrey against the brightening sky. The three peaks which were visible to him seemed to rise abruptly from the gentle upslope of the rolling country where he'd stopped for the night.

Now Longarm began to wonder how much further he'd have to travel, but with only the knowledge that Don Carlos O'Riley's ranch was somewhere ahead of him, he realized that an estimate or even a guess would be nothing more than a shot in the dark. He knew too well how some trails ran in loops and zigzags, adding miles to distances which to the eye appeared very short.

Lighting his after-breakfast cigar, Longarm saddled the horse and levered himself onto its back. He reined the animal to the trail and began riding north, ignoring the complaints of his scantily filled stomach. He'd been moving across the rising country for perhaps two hours when he reached a point in the trail where it forked abruptly at the bank of a small stream.

Longarm reined in and sat studying the two branches of the dimly marked path. By this time the sun climbing the sky had warmed the air and he was very much aware of the reminders his stomach was sending him that too long a time had passed since his scanty breakfast.

"Well, now, old son," Longarm told himself, speaking aloud to break the silence. "The fellow in the bank you asked about getting to this Don Carlos O'Riley's place said to take the right-hand fork, so that's what you better do."

Touching his toe to the horse's flank, Longarm reined the animal along the stream bank. After he'd covered a mile or a bit more he felt hungrier than ever.

"You was in too big a rush to get outa Monterrey, old son," he muttered. "You shoulda picked up more supplies."

Then Longarm fell silent when he caught sight of a small cluster of buildings standing in a higgledy-piggledy scatter just off the trail ahead. As he got closer to them and saw that they were built with bits and pieces of weathered wood and scraps of tin, his first impression was that they were abandoned, and he shook his head unhappily. Then he saw a thin trail of smoke rising from the hut nearest the road, and his vexation vanished.

By the time he'd reached the first of the little structures Longarm could see other wisps of smoke curling from the stovepipe chimneys of two or three of the huts that were well back from the trail. He turned his horse toward them, and when he'd reached the nearest of the little huts he reined in.

At close range he could see the crude sign on its side. *"Baratas y baños,"* it read. Although his command of Spanish was marginal, Longarm had worked enough cases in Mexico to be able to translate the words: "Bargains and Baths." He dismounted and stepped through the shanty's open door. The interior of the little hut was dim, and Longarm stopped just inside, blinking in the semi-darkness.

"Bienvenido, señor," a man's voice greeted him from the half-darkness at the rear of the room. *"Acquello que quieres?"*

Longarm did not even try to reply in Spanish. He asked, "You talk English any?"

"I e-speak a leetle," the dimly visible man replied. "What ees eet you weesh?"

"Why, I'm hoping you can sell me something to eat, maybe some sausage or cheese or bread or *tortillas*," Longarm replied. "I'm hungry enough so's I'll be right glad to buy most any kind of grub you've got on hand."

"Queso y tortillas, sí," the man replied. "From my house I weel need to get theem for you."

"Suppose you just do that before we palaver any more" Longarm suggested. "I'll wait right here, and while I'm having a bite maybe you can tell me a little bit about where I am and where that road outside is going to take me."

"De seguro," the storekeeper answered. He started toward the door. "But I can e-see you have the hungry. We can talk after I have bring back from my house the food."

As the storekeeper passed him heading for the door, Longarm got his first close look at the man and saw that he had only one arm. His right arm ended at the elbow. He was gone before Longarm could say anything more, and Longarm turned his attention to the scanty stock spread out on the three tables that filled the little one-room building.

There was very little for him to look at. One table was covered with a clutter of battered and bent pots and pans. Another held rusting hand tools, hammers and shovels and chisels that were suffering from long use and misuse, while the third bore a miscellany of chipped and cracked pottery and chinaware: cups, saucers, a bowl or two, and a few plates.

Longarm was just finishing his cursory inspection when the proprietor returned. He was carrying a pottery plate which held a large chunk of white cheese resting on a small stack of *tortillas*. He offered the plate to Longarm, who wasted no time in breaking off a piece of the cheese and wrapping it in one of the tortillas. He was still chewing when he realized that he had not offered to pay the storekeeper.

"If you'll tell me what I owe you, I'll settle up soon as I get through eating," Longarm said after swallowing his first bite. "But I was so hungry I got forgetful. I didn't even wait long enough to say thanks."

"De nada," the storekeeper said with a shrug. "Eet ees easy to see you are honest man, even eef I have not before seen you. Where do you go?"

Longarm had already bitten off another chunk of cheese and a piece of *tortilla*. He hurried his chewing and swallowed before replying. "I'm looking for a ranch that a fellow named Carlos O'Riley's got someplace close around here. I reckon you'd know just exactly where it is."

"Seguramente," the storekeeper nodded. "Everybody ees know Don Carlos and hees Rancho Miraflores. Ees close to here, bot from trail *ahí* ees not to see." Gesturing now with the stub-arm, he went on. "You e-stay on trail to leetle pond, then go past pond, you are there find trail branch. Go up new trail to top and theen you weel e-see the *hacienda* of Don Carlos. Ees beeg *casa*. You weel see it from far away."

"Well, I'm sure glad to get straightened out about where I got to go," Longarm said. "I guess you'd know how much of a ride it is from here?"

"A small e-way, ees not afar."

"Less'n an hour's ride, would you say?"

"Una hora," the storekeeper said. *"Al pasado,* wheen I am e-work for Don Carlos, I am never to hurry."

"You were one of the hands on his ranch?" Longarm asked.

"Four, five years I am *vaquero* for heem." As he spoke the storekeeper raised the stub that remained of his right arm and jerked his head toward the infirmity. "Wheen weeth my *riata* I am clomsy and e-lose thees hand, I can no more be *vaquero*. Ees theen Don Carlos geeve me thees land, thees e-store."

"So I reckon you sorta think pretty highly of him?"

After a long moment of hesitation the merchant said, "Don Carlos, he ees es not same man now as was theen."

From the manner in which the storekeeper spoke, choosing his words carefully, Longarm realized that there was more left unsaid than had been said. "You're saying he's changed since you had to quit working for him?"

After a moment of thoughtful silence the storekeeper replied, "Wheen I am work for Don Carlos, he was *solamente* ranchero. *Ahora,* ees beeg man, *importante,* ees e-spend more time weeth *los ricos* een Monterrey as on *rancho,* ees leave *la señora* alone for long times. I am see heem ride by, he ees not wave, ees not e-stop."

"Too busy to pay any mind to you, is he?"

"Thees ees so. Ees like now he no longer ees *ranchero,* but ees from *los politicos, los ricos, los . . .*" The man's voice trailed off as he shook his head sadly.

Longarm's past experiences in questioning reluctant individuals told him that the time had passed when he could expect the storekeeper to tell him more. He swallowed the last bite of the cheese and *tortillas* and reached into his pocket.

"How much do I owe you?" he asked.

"You do not owe me a *centavo, señor.*"

Longarm was already looking at the handful of loose change he'd dug from his pocket. He picked a half dollar from the little scramble of coins and extended the coin. "What I ate came right off your table and that's money outa your pocket. Now, you'll do me a favor by taking this four-bit piece. It don't come outa my pocket. When I'm working away from home I get paid back later on for whatever I've spent."

"Thees es true?" the storekeeper asked.

"True as anything can be," Longarm assured him. He pushed the coin into the storekeeper's hand, and this time the man accepted it. Longarm went on. "And I thank you for helping me, too. Now I got to be moving along."

"Pues, vaya con Dios, señor."

Longarm nodded and turned to go. He swung into the saddle and rode back to the trail. Ahead the ground rose steadily, and the little stream beside the path was now dancing in white splashes over the stones that formed its bottom. Again, Longarm let the horse set its own gait. He'd had been in the saddle for an hour or so when the rivulet beside the trail became a small still-water pond.

Reining in, Longarm scanned the area around him. He could see that the trail divided in two beyond the pond and that one branch led up the rise and vanished over its crest. Nudging his horse with his boot toe, he turned at the trail fork and started up the gentle slope.

When he reached the top of the rise, Longarm reined in again. A short distance ahead, midway on a long gentle downslope, the trail ended abruptly at a barb-wire fence. Beyond the fence the ground was well-grazed pastureland, dotted with the hoof marks of steers and their droppings. In the distance Longarm could see a small herd of cattle grazing. He could tell that they were Mexican cattle by the deep brown of their coats and the broad span of their horns.

"Well, now old son," Longarm said into the quiet air, "looks like these folks in Mexico's getting smart. It used to be that you'd never see a herd of steers, let alone

79

a fence, south of the border. But maybe it's just that this Don Carlos O'Riley's smarter than most. Anyways, wherever there's steers inside of a fence, there's got to be a gate of some kind. Thing to do is find it."

Longarm toed his horse into motion again. As he drew closer to the fence he could see that there'd be no need to wonder which direction to choose, for the trail outside the barbwire strands showed much more evidence of travel to the right than it did to the left. He reined his horse away from the fence, taking the most-used direction, and sat back comfortably in his saddle, keeping to the same slow pace that had marked his approach.

When Longarm reached the end of the barbwire enclosure, where the fence angled abruptly down the gentle slope, he saw a thread of smoke against the bright sky, and that the trail he was following curved toward it. Since it was only sign of human habitation that he'd seen, Longarm turned his horse toward the almost invisible smoke thread.

He'd ridden only a short way when the land beside the trail suddenly dropped away. It seemed to stretch across an endless expanse of verdant, gently rolling plains to a new and lower horizon. However, it was not the view of the land that held Longarm's attention. He kept his eyes fixed on the elaborate mansion that rose from the level prairie a short distance from the crest where he'd stopped. It was a glistening white structure three stories high, with a facade of pillars and a broad veranda extending across its imposing width.

"Well, now, old son," Longarm said aloud, his voice sounding strange to him in the quiet morning air. "It looks like you finally got to where you're headed for."

Settling back in his saddle, Longarm fingered one of his long thin cigars from his pocket and lighted it as he studied the mansion and the outbuildings that clustered near it. Beyond the mansion there were a number of smaller buildings, and even at a distance Longarm was positive that they were for the household staff. It was obvious that such a large and impressive mansion would require a sizeable number of servants.

Beyond the big main building stables formed a long narrow line; opposite them were blank-faced boxy structures that would be used for storage. Further away, past the mansion and its outbuildings, the land was dotted by small houses that were obviously the quarters of the sizeable army of hands that must be needed to keep the entire ranch functioning.

Through the smoke from his cigar Longarm told himself, "Now this has got to be the place the fellow that fed you breakfast told you about, old son. Sure as God made little green apples, it's got to belong to this Don Carlos O'Riley, because it's about as fancy as that bank of his you saw back in Monterrey. And that can add up to one of just two things. Either he's rich enough to buy about anything he takes a fancy to, or he's spending so much money here and on the bank that he's always having to scramble for the hard cold cash he's got to dig up to keep both of 'em going."

Tossing away the butt of his cigar, Longarm started his horse down the trail that led to the house. The closer he got to it the more imposing the mansion became. It seemed to grow wider and the line of columns that supported the eaves of the roof that projected across the narrow portico appeared to increase in size. Beyond the pillars the front of the house was broken by wide windows, their line interrupted only by the double doors of its entryway.

"A man'd have to be rich as sin to keep this big of a place going," Longarm said to himself as he drew closer to the mansion and looked along the ground in front of it for a place where he could tether his horse, but he saw no hitching post or rail. "It's funny they ain't got a place out in front here where folks that stop by for a visit can leave a horse."

Almost before Longarm had finished speaking the door of the imposing mansion swung open and a man came out. For a moment Longarm thought that the man might be Don Carlos O'Riley himself. Then he realized that the proprietor of such an elaborate establishment would not be wearing the baggy unpressed white jacket and trousers of the man now walking toward him, nor would Don Carlos be coming to greet an arriving stranger.

"*Bienvenido, señor,*" the man said as he reached Longarm and stopped. "I am Andres, the *mayordomo* of El Rancho Miraflores. I must ask you why you are here, what eet ees your business."

"If this is where a fellow named Carlos O'Riley lives, it's him I come to see," Longarm answered.

"You are e-friend of Don Carlos? He ees perhaps espect you to arrive?"

"Now, I can't give you any sorta answer to what you've asked me," Longarm replied. "My business with him's sorta private. But if it wasn't important, I sure wouldn't't've ridden all the way here to see him. I missed him in Monterrey, and none of the folks at that bank of his had any idea about when he'd be back, so I just headed on out here."

"And your business weeth heem? Eet is what?"

"I ain't meaning to give you no short answer, but my business here ain't with you. It's important business with your boss," Longarm said.

"Of thees, I do not dispute, *señor,*" Andres replied. "Bot eet ees my duty to ask of those who come here

82

why they are weesh to speak with *el patron.*"

Keeping his voice level but firm, Longarm went on. "It sorta looks like you and me has both got bosses. Now, my boss has sent me here to talk to your boss, and I've ridden a long ways to do just that. I ain't about to tell you any more'n what I have already, so suppose you just kite inside and let him know I need to have a little talk with him."

For a moment, the *mayordomo* frowned as he considered Longarm's request. At last he nodded and said, "For you to travel soch a long way, your business weeth Don Carlos most be important, so thees thing I weel do. You weel e-please wait here while I am go to ask."

"Sure," Longarm said. "Take your time. Now that I've got here, I ain't in no more of a hurry."

Settling back into his saddle, Longarm watched the man as he disappeared into the mansion. After he'd waited for several minutes he lighted a fresh cigar. He'd been puffing at it long enough to reduce its length by almost an inch, and his patience was beginning to ebb, when the door of the big house opened and the *mayordomo* emerged. He held the entry door open and Longarm's eyes widened when he saw the woman who followed him.

Even at a distance Longarm got the immediate impression that she was both young and beautiful. She wore a flowing white dress which hid her figure and an elaborately embroidered *mantilla* draped over her head and shoulders. The scarf revealed a rim of shining black hair and as she approached the details of her face became clearer. It was a perfect oval from brow to chin: ink-black eyes framed by thick dark lashes and eyebrows, an aquiline nose, full crimson lips, and a firm but not obtrusive chin.

Behind her and a bit to one side Andres followed the woman. A few paces from Longarm he stepped ahead of her, as though to protect her, and said, "Thees ees la Señora Adelita. She ees wife of Don Carlos, she weel e-speak for heem. Since he is not here, you can tell her your business with heem." Turning to the woman, he said, "I have told you all I know of thees man who e-say hees business weeth *el patron* ees *muy importante*. Perhaps you will tell heem what ees best to do."

Longarm spoke quickly, before the woman could say anything. "Your man there's giving you the straight of it, ma'am. My name's Long. Custis Long. I got real important business with your husband, and I've ridden a long ways to talk to him. Maybe you can tell me when he'll be back?"

"I only wish that I could give you an answer to your question," she replied. Her English was both unaccented and flawless. "However, Carlos does not always tell me his plans."

"Well, now, I can understand why a busy man might not have time to do much talking, but you oughta have some idea about where he might've been going," Longarm said.

"It is usual that I know," she said with a frown. "But in the late hours of last night a messenger rode in. He must have brought important news, for Carlos left with him at once. He did not even take time to tell me where he was going."

"He didn't want to bother you, the hour being what it was, I guess," Longarm suggested.

"Yes, I'm sure that's what it was," Adelita agreed. "But now that you've traveled all the way here to see him, I'm sure that he would wish to speak with you. Please, dismount and let Andres put your horse in our stables while you come inside with me. Together we will visit and talk while you wait for Carlos to return."

Chapter 8

Longarm had been studying Adelita O'Riley unobtrusively, confirming his first impression of her. He was so surprised when he heard the invitation that for a moment he could only sit speechless in his saddle. Then he dismounted and stood holding the reins of his livery horse.

"I hope you ain't got the idea that I was hinting around for an invite like you gave me, Miz O'Riley," he said. "I can just as easy ride a little ways off and find me a place . . .".

She stopped him with a gesture, a flick of her hand, and when Longarm stopped talking she went on, "The invitation is on behalf of my husband. I understand that the business you have with Carlos must be important, or you would not have traveled such a great distance to see him."

"You sure hit that nail square on the head, ma'am," Longarm assured her.

"Since I am not sure exactly where he has gone, I cannot send a messenger to tell him you are here. He could have returned to Monterrey, or he could have gone to the mine up in Las Cumbres, but I know that he would wish for you to wait so that he can discuss with you this matter of business you have with him."

"Now, I'd be right sure he didn't go to Monterrey, because that's where I started from," Longarm said. "If he'd been heading back there, I'd've run into him on the road."

"Then I'm sure he's gone to the mine in las Cumbres," she said. "It is not far, and he will quite likely return by this evening. And as I said a moment ago, he will wish to see you."

"Not any more'n I want to see him," Longarm agreed. "I got a real hankering to meet up with him, because we're due to have a good long palaver."

"Then I'm sure you must agree that it would be most inhospitable for me to allow you to leave the Rancho Miraflores before my husband returns."

"From what you said a minute ago, he might not be back right soon," Longarm reminded her. "And I don't expect you'd want me being underfoot for very long."

"Time is of small importance here," she assured him with a smile. "We pay little attention to it, except when we have the *rodeo de ganado,* what you would call the roundup."

"Well, now," Longarm said hesitantly, "I got to admit it'd be easier for me to set and wait than to go poking around in country I don't know much about, but I don't want to be putting you to a lot of trouble."

"It will not inconvenience me for you to stay. On the contrary, I would welcome having someone besides my maid and the house servants to talk with."

"If you're sure that's the way you want it, then I won't argue with you," Longarm said.

"So. We will consider it settled," Adelita said. Turning to the *mayordomo,* she went on. "Our guest will go into the house with me, Andres. Before you join us, you will need to tell one of your stable hands to attend to his horse. And as you go to the stables, please stop at the kitchen and tell *la cocinera* to send us refreshments, *bizcochos, cafe, tequila . . .*" Breaking off, she turned to Longarm. "So many of your countrymen do not like our drinks such as *tequila* and *aquardiente* that we keep your country's whiskey for visitors. Perhaps you would prefer it?"

"Well, ma'am, a cup of hot coffee'd be plenty good enough for me," Longarm replied. "But seeing as how you got it on hand, I wouldn't turn down something stronger to go with the coffee. Maybe a swallow of Maryland rye whiskey, if it ain't too much trouble."

"None at all," she assured him. To Andres she said, "You have heard. Tell one of the housemaids to bring the whiskey for our guest, and for me the *aguardiente de Napoleon,* as well as coffee for both of us."

"*De seguro, señora,*" Andres said. "I weel see to it."

Andres started toward the mansion and Adelita returned her attention to Longarm. "Let us go now to the house," she said. "I'm sure that you will be glad to sit in a chair instead of a saddle, or on the bare ground. I know how tiring the ride here is from Monterrey."

"Oh, I've made a lot worse trips than the one I had getting here," Longarm told her as they started toward the ranch house. "But I got to admit, it'll be nice to stop for a while." They took a few more steps. "I'd reckon your husband's a pretty busy man these days, with that big bank he's got in Monterrey. And I'd make a guess that he's into a lot of other businesses that I don't know anything about."

"It's true that the bank requires much of his attention." she agreed. "And the mine in Las Cumbres is taking much more of Carlos's time as well, so that I am alone a great deal. But I have the flowers and the *hacienda* to look after. It's true that the *criadas* do the work, but I must keep looking after them to make sure it is done properly. That alone is enough to keep me busy."

Longarm's attention had been aroused before when Adelita O'Riley first mentioned that there was a mine in the mountains to the north. He'd managed to keep his surprise from showing on his face, and also succeeded in suppressing his immediate urge to begin asking questions. Now acknowledging her words with a nod, he turned his attention to examining the imposing bulk of the mansion they were approaching.

They had been walking slowly toward the house during their brief conversation, and when they reached the door Adelita pushed it open a bit wider. She stepped inside with a gesture indicating that Longarm was to follow her. His jaw dropped when he saw the size of the room he'd entered.

Its dimensions were those of a ballroom, and its ceiling was unusually high, dwarfing the elaborate furnishings and the walls of mirrors that spanned each end. Large crystal chandeliers hung from the ceiling, which was decorated with an elaborate design. The floor was of highly polished hardwood and the clicking of his boot heels started echoes that resounded in the huge room.

Longarm followed his guide across the oceanic space into an adjoining chamber. This was a dining room that matched in size the room they'd just left. Three wide mahogany tables spanned the room's length, and still left room for sideboards and narrow serving-tables and storage cabinets for dishes and glasses along the walls.

Adelita did not stop as they went through the first two enormously large chambers, and Longarm had only a little time to observe their details. Then he followed his hostess from the dining room into a third room. It was fully carpeted and furnished for meals on a family-sized scale. There was a small oval table and a half-dozen chairs, and a narrow sideboard and china cabinet hugged the wall flanking a door.

Flicking his eyes around the room as they passed through it, Longarm began to feel more at home. Finally they entered a fourth room, smaller in its dimensions than the others he'd passed through. From its more modest size and furnishings, a small table and a half-dozen chairs, he guessed it was a family sitting room.

Adelita gestured toward a chair, and as Longarm moved toward it she settled down into another chair close by. "I could not but notice you examining our formal rooms," she said. "With our country upset by one revolution following swiftly after another, we use them but seldom now, and I will confess that at times they cause me to wonder about what they must have seen when our land was peaceful."

"Well, I got to admit those big rooms we came through sure knock a man's eyes out," Longarm replied as he sat down in the chair Adelita had indicated. "What size of a place is this ranch anyhow?"

"It would take a very long time for me to tell you," she answered. "But you must understand that the *hacienda* was first started many years ago, when the *ricos* used the *peones* as slaves. It was a very small *rancho* then, but my husband and his father before him kept building until now it is very large indeed. And such elaborate places as this are no longer being built in Mexico. Things have changed since the revolutions started."

"Oh, sure," Longarm agreed. "But—"

Their conversation was interrupted by a maid bringing in a tray that held cups, saucers, and a coffeepot as well as a small plate containing a stack of thick wafers. Another maid followed, and on her tray there were two bottles and two glasses. They placed the trays on a table and looked questioningly at Adelita. She nodded toward the door and the maids left the room at once.

"We will be able to talk with greater ease than would be the case if they stayed to serve us," Adelita said. "But I must ask you to pour your own drink while I serve the coffee."

Longarm glanced at the bottles on the tray Adelita had indicated. One was labeled *Aguardiente,* the second Old Mark Rye Whiskey. Though he'd never encountered the whiskey label before, Longarm had no taste for the generally sweetened Mexican brandy. He picked up the bottle of whiskey, poured a small amount into a glass, and tasted it. It lacked the full bite of his favorite rye, but it was passable. He filled the glass and settled back in his chair.

While Longarm was still swallowing his first experimental sip of the unfamiliar whiskey, Adelita stepped up to the table beside him and put a tray on the table before sitting down next to him. She said, "I hope you find our whiskey suits your taste, Señor Long. We keep it only for visitors such as you, who prefer it to our Mexican liquors."

"Why, it fills the bill fine, ma'am," Longarm assured her. "But I didn't expect for you to go to a lot of trouble on my account."

"Hospitality to strangers is our way here in Mexico," she said. "But you will know this if you have been to our country before."

"I've been here a time or two," Longarm answered. "Mostly on business."

"Your business has to do with cattle?"

"Sometimes with cattle, sometimes with other things." Longarm took another swallow of his drink as Adelita turned to the tray holding the coffeepot and started to fill one of the cups. Then he went on. "A minute ago, ma'am, you said something about your husband maybe going to a mine up in the mountains. If you could tell me how to locate it, I'd go looking for him and save myself some time and spare you having me underfoot while I'm waiting for him to come back here."

"You would surely not wish to travel further today, after riding from Monterrey," she said. She set a cup of coffee in front of Longarm before continuing. "And even though Las Cumbres are not great in size, the trails in them are sometimes very faint. They are not easy to follow."

"Now, ma'am, I've followed more trails than I can count," Longarm said. "All you'd need to do is show me where it starts, and it ain't likely I'll loose it."

"Your skill I do not question, Señor Long," Adelita assured him. "It is my lacking of knowledge that gives me doubt. I would be very much afraid that if I tried to tell you of the trails you would have trouble, since I am not really familiar myself with the new trail to the mine. But I am positive that Carlos will surely be back late today—tomorrow at the latest."

"Well, that ain't long enough of a wait to make much never-mind," Longarm assured her. "And I got to thank you right now for putting me up tonight. While that's on

91

my mind, I guess I can beg a bath and some hot water to shave with before supper. I got the trail-dust itchies and I got a pretty good idea of what I look like right now, after making a two-day ride here from Monterrey."

"I will tell one of the maids to prepare a bath for you," Adelita said. "And one of them will show you to the room which will be yours tonight. Breakfast will be waiting for you at daybreak. and if Carlos has not returned by them, Andres will guide you to the beginning of the trail that will take you into Las Cumbres."

"Well, ma'am, I sure do thank you for all the looking-after you're giving me," Longarm told her as he stood up. "And if you'll excuse me, I'll just go along right now and get shed of my trail dust and my whiskers before supper."

"Of course," she said. "You will hear the bell, or better still, I will send one of the house servants to knock on your door and show you to the dining room."

"Now, that's real thoughtful," Longarm said. "And I do thank you for all the trouble you're taking on my account. I'll just go along and get spruced up a bit so I'll be ready when the dinner bell rings."

Sunrise found Longarm following the faintly marked trail to which he'd been led by the ranch foreman in the first gray tinges of the day's beginning dawn. Ahead of him the low, bluntly undulating peaks of the three low mountains called Las Cumbres broke the steadily brightening skyline. His rested horse was moving steadily along the gentle upgrade, and even in the dawn's dimness he had little trouble in following the trail to which he'd been guided by Andres.

With the first pink tinges of sunrise appearing now on the eastern horizon he could see details more clearly. It was easier now, for Longarm to tell that the trail was much newer than the one he'd taken at the edge of the O'Riley ranch. He could also see that virtually all of the hoofprints on the new trail had been made by the small hooves of burros instead of the bigger hooves of horses.

"Old son," Longarm said under his breath, his words sounding loud in the quiet air, "a man'd have to be blind if he couldn't just look at how deep and sharp those little burro-prints are and not be able to figure out the critters that made 'em were carrying about all the load they could handle."

He was silent for a few thoughtful moments, then spoke again. "Now about the heaviest thing those burros could be toting is gold pieces, but most likely it's brass or copper that's been coated with gold, the way Billy Vail told you these outlaws are doing. They'd be real close to weighing about as much as gold does. You know, old son, it sorta looks like you've picked up the trail you been trying to find ever since you got away from them murdering *rurales*."

Toeing his horse ahead, Longarm held it to a walk as he continued his slow progress, keeping his eyes on the trail. Though there were long stretches of hard-baked earth where the hoofprints were faint, the land had little variety. Everywhere he looked his surroundings were hard-crusted soil broken only by the rise of an occasional protruding shelf and now and then a massive boulder.

One of the big masses of stone loomed just ahead of him, and Longarm looped the reins of his mount around his saddlehorn while he fished out a cigar and clamped it in his jaws. He was flicking his thumbnail across a match head as the horse reached the huge rock outcrop and started around it. As the match flared into flame Longarm cupped it in his hands, and took his eyes off his surroundings while he bent his head to puff the stogie's tip into a glow.

When he raised his head Longarm found himself staring into the muzzle of a rifle, aimed at him and held unwaveringly by a horseman who had suddenly appeared from beyond the jutting curve of the high stone buttress. The man holding the rifle wore the ornate clothing favored by Mexico's higher classes: a dun-hued felt sombrero gleaming with gold-braid ornamentation, a short-sleeved vest crusted with more gold braid, bottom-flared trousers, and shining calf-high boots. Longarm had no doubt that the horseman was Don Carlos O'Riley.

"Raise your arms and do not move them," the rider said before Longarm could speak. His voice was almost casual, but it carried the tone of a man accustomed to commanding. "You die if you do not do as I say!"

Longarm had no choice but to obey. He dropped the reins and lifted his arms, being careful not to make any sort of gesture that the man with the rifle might take as a threat.

"Umberto!" the man called without taking his eyes off Longarm "*Vente 'ca y tome del extranjero su fusil!*"

A second man emerged from behind the protruding stone formation. He wore the loose cotton trousers and jacket which constituted the garb of the *mayordomo* at the Rancho Miraflores. He paid no attention to the man who'd given the orders, but stepped up to Longarm's mount and reached to grasp Longarm's Winchester.

"*Tome también su pistola!*" the mounted man commanded.

This was not the first time Longarm had heard such orders. He decided quickly that at the present moment his best course was to do nothing, then bluff his way out and gamble on his bluff being successful, even if it meant delaying any efforts he might make to free himself. He did not move when the man who'd taken his rifle stepped along the side of the horse and lifted Longarm's Colt from its holster. Carrying the weapons, the man stepped back behind the horseman who'd been giving the orders.

"Now," the rider said, "you will tell me who you are, why you are on my land, and where you have come from as well as where you are going. And I warn you now, let your words be truthful."

"Long's my name. Custis Long. And from what I gather by the way you been acting and talking, you'd be Don Carlos O'Riley. If you are, you're the man I got business with."

"I am indeed Carlos O'Riley," the horseman said. "But your name I have not heard before. What is this business matter you say you wish to discuss with me?"

"That's something I figure we'd best put off till we get to some place where nobody else is around," Longarm replied. "I'll leave it up to you to say whether we move away from this man you got with you to some place far enough from him so we can talk private, or wait till we get back to that big ranch house of yours."

O'Riley's jaw dropped as he stared amazed at Longarm, but he recovered quickly. He asked, "You have been to the Rancho Miraflores?"

"Well, now, that was the only place I knew where to look for you," Longarm said. "Before I started out for it, I stopped at your bank in Monterrey and the man there said you'd already left to go back to your ranch. Now, I didn't figure I'd have much of a chance catching up with you, so I done what anybody else'd do. I went looking for

95

you at your home place. When I got there, Miz O'Riley told me you'd likely be up here in the hills, so I come looking for you."

Even before Longarm finished his explanation, O'Riley had recovered from his surprise. The amazement that had been showing on his face became one of anger.

"You lie!" he snapped. "Adelita would not be so foolish!"

Longarm realized two things immediately. The first was that he had made a serious mistake when he mentioned the part played by Adelita O'Riley in setting him on the trail into the mountains. The second was that as long as O'Riley was in such an obvious rage, the rancher's treatment of him would be unpredictable. Though he had little hope of being able to deceive his captor for more than a very short time, Longarm made the best effort he could muster under the circumstances.

"Now look here, Mr. O'Riley," he said. "I got business to talk with you, and this sure ain't no good way to start out. If you'll just—"

"I will do what I think best!" O'Riley told him. "It is not my way to take a risk which I can avoid. We will go back to a place where no one will disturb us." Without taking his eyes off Longarm, he raised his voice and called, "*Volvemos a la mina! Umberto, cuidarte el extranjero!*"

Chapter 9

Longarm said nothing when the man whom O'Riley had addressed as Umberto pulled a saddle string from Longarm's mount, and when he began lashing Longarm's wrists to his saddlehorn, both experience and common sense told Longarm not to resist. He watched silently while Umberto looped the saddle strings of his own horse to tie the Colt and Winchester, then removed the lariat that was hanging from its saddlehorn.

Longarm's poker skill had taught him the art of keeping his face inscrutable. His expression did not change when Umberto stepped back and looped the lariat's noose around his neck. Instead, he acted as though being treated like a prisoner was a routine everyday experience. Umberto adjusted the loop, drawing it tightly enough to choke if Longarm should try to leap from the saddle, but loose enough to be bearable. Then he stepped back and turned to face O'Riley.

"*Ahorita no evadirese, patron,*" he said, indicating Longarm with a gesture. "*Que hacemos ahorita?*"

"*Volvemos a la factoría,*" the rancher replied. "*El prisionero sera seguro ahi.*"

Longarm frowned, intrigued by the exchange between O'Riley and Umberto. His knowledge of Spanish was limited and he could not be sure that he'd understood their exchange completely. He was especially interested in the word *factoría*. He could think of at least one reason for a factory in a location so far from the main ranch house.

Even before Umberto was secure in his saddle, O'Riley had turned his mount back in the direction from which he had been coming. As Umberto moved to take a position behind O'Riley, Longarm's eyes were drawn to his Winchester and gunbelt secured to the cantle of Umberto's saddle.

Shaking his head unhappily, he muttered under his breath, "Old son, them guns are what you need right now. But you got about as much chance as a snowball in Hell of getting your hands on 'em, at least for now. And this O'Riley fellow ain't no fool. Sure as God made little green apples, he ain't about to give you no chance to get 'em, so you better be figuring out how to make your own chance."

When they reached the end of the long gentle curve of the narrow trail, Longarm saw a half-dozen burros strung out along the ledge. The little animals were hitched together by lengths of rope and each of them had a humped canvas-covered load on its back. The burros were small; their rumps were below the shoulder level of the men who'd been standing beside them and who were now tugging vigorously on the animals' lead ropes as they struggled to turn the burros around on the narrow shelf.

Behind Umberto and Longarm, Carlos O'Riley's voice rose in a shout. *"Cuidarse, quiero pasar!"*

Umberto reined his horse as close as possible to the drop off side of the trail. The men wrangling the burros pushed and tugged the loaded animals to the opposite side and pushed them to the base of the cliff. O'Riley managed to squeeze past them, his horse's hooves within inches of the edge of the narrow trail.

Umberto followed his employer's example, leading Longarm's horse along the ticklishly narrow strip between the line of burros and the drop-off of the ledge. When O'Riley reached the end of the laden burros and resumed his place at what was now the head of the little procession, he waved for the others to follow him. As Umberto and Longarm caught up with him, Umberto called to his employer.

"Hola, patron," he said *"Es necesario que tomemos los burros? Son muy agobiados."*

Shaking his head, O'Riley answered, *"Tomemos no riesgo, Umberto. El tesoro sale con nosotros."*

Umberto did not argue. He accepted his employer's decision to keep the laden burros with them and continued leading Longarm along the winding pathway. After a moment or two Longarm glanced back and saw that the *burros* were following them. Soon the slanting grade began to level out and the trail widened. O'Riley began setting a faster pace and Umberto speeded up as well. They reached the end of the ledge and Longarm turned his attention to the land ahead.

In the broad, shallow, half-circular valley that was now fully visible below the line of hills, Longarm saw several sprawled huddles of small adobe huts. They stood in little clumps and clusters, dwarfed by the two buildings beyond them. These were substantial structures, with walls and roofs of corrugated iron. Both of the large buildings had chimneys or smokestacks rising from their roofs.

Even at a distance Longarm could see that paths had been worn from the small dwellings to the buildings. A trickle of smoke was rising from one of the shorter chimneys of the largest of the two structures, but there was no sign of life in the area around them. Longarm had seen similar buildings before and recognized their purpose.

"Well, old son, if that ain't a smelting plant, you never did see one," he told himself silently. "And its a pretty good-sized one, too. Now, a man don't need to do much guessing about what it's for, and that those fake gold coins are what comes outa it. But taking care of that place has got to wait till you can figure out a way to get outa this jackpot you've got caught in. It likely won't be too long before you'll have your chance, so the sooner you figure out what to do, the easier it'll be to make your move when the time comes."

For a moment or two Longarm scanned the shallow oval valley, looking for any of its features which might be useful to him when he'd succeeded in escaping from O'Riley's men. Even though he still had to work out the time and method of regaining his freedom, he had no doubt at all that he'd manage to break free. His inspection gave him scant encouragement. There were a few people moving around the clustered huts, but everywhere else he looked the valley's floor was covered with short grasses which were too thin to be used as either concealment or shelter.

Longarm resumed his silent colloquy. "Looks like there ain't much you can do but wait and see what's up ahead, old son. It's going to take a mite of figuring, but more'n likely there ain't more'n two or three men around those smelter buildings, and there'll be time enough to handle that part of the job after you come up with some ideas about how the odds stand. Right this minute there ain't nobody in this valley that's on your side, so the first thing you got to do is find a way to change that."

While Longarm had been taking stock of his surroundings the little group had been moving steadily across the floor of the vast round valley. O'Riley had kept his position at the head of the small procession. When they reached the nearest of the two buildings he reined in at its wide-open door, and was lifting himself in his stirrups, getting ready to dismount, when a tall cadaverous man stepped out of the building.

Longarm frowned when he saw the man. There was something familiar about the newcomer that started him searching his memory.

"I wasn't looking for you back so soon," the newcomer said to O'Riley. "What'd you do, run into trouble on the trail?"

Hearing the man's voice gave Longarm the memory link that he'd needed. Now he recognized the newcomer as a drifter he'd once arrested. A moment of thoughtful mind-searching brought up the man's name—Jim Timmons. Satisfied, Longarm returned his full attention to the conversation that had begun between Timmons and O'Riley.

"I have come back to tell you that we must make a small change in our plans," the *hacendado* was saying. He had settled back into his saddle when Timmons appeared. Now he jerked his head back toward Longarm. "I have not the time to spend questioning this man, and I do not wish to take him to the Rancho Miraflores."

"What's that got to do with me?" Timmons asked. He'd been glancing at Longarm now and then, but had shown no sign that he'd recognized him.

"You will lock him in one of the small storerooms" O'Riley said. "I must go back to Monterrey at once, but my stay there will be short. When I return, I will find out why this stranger has come here. Until then you will be responsible for keeping him."

A frown had grown on Timmons' face while O'Riley talked. Now Timmons said, "Wait just a minute, Don Carlos! You hired me on to run this smelter, not mess into your private business. Standing guard over somebody you got a grudge with sure ain't part of my job!"

"While I am employing you you will do as I say!" O'Riley snapped. "But for your trouble in guarding this man, you will be given extra pay." Timmons opened his mouth to reply, but the rancher was already twisting in his saddle to address Umberto. He gestured toward Longarm. *"Asisterle. Conoces que quiero hacer."*

"Sí, patron," Umberto replied. He dismounted and started toward Longarm.

"Now, hold on!" Longarm protested. "You're making too much of a howdy-do outa me being here! There sure ain't no reason for you to lock me away like I was out to steal from you! If you'll just take the time to listen—"

"Callate!" O'Riley shouted. "Be quiet! You are like all your countrymen, you think we Mexicanos are stupid!" He turned to Umberto. *"Tome el gringo por dentro. Sobre volvemos al rancho, decidemos cualquier es necesario."*

Longarm's knowledge of Spanish was not extensive, but he had been able to grasp the gist of the exchanges between O'Riley and Umberto. He opened his mouth to protest further, but before he had time to speak he realized that anything he said would be ignored. He also realized that he'd been on the brink of making a serious mistake by revealing his true identity.

O'Riley waited for a moment, then said, "There is no need for you to say more." Turning to Timmons, he said, "You will guard this man closely, do you understand? I would be very angry if he is not here when we return."

"It's easy enough for you to talk about me guarding him," Timmons replied. "But I guess you recall that you taken away my pistol when I begun working for you. Now how in hell am I gonna get this fellow to toe the line if I ain't got a gun to back up what I tell him to do?"

O'Riley was silent for a moment. Then he nodded and said, "Though I do not trust you *norteamericanos,* there is no harm you can do if I allow you to have a weapon here. I can understand that you may indeed need a gun." He turned to Umberto. "Leave the prisoner's weapons and his saddlebags here with Timmons. They would only be in our way if we carry them to the *hacienda.*"

"You got any idee when you'll be coming back?" Timmons asked as Umberto moved to obey O'Riley's command. "I reckon you'll recall what I told you before you taken off the first time, about me starting to run short of grub. And even if I put this fellow here in a storeroom, I got to feed him."

"I do not forget such things," O'Riley replied. "And I will see that food is sent from the *rancho* at once. Until it arrives, get what you need from *los poblachos.*"

"Why, the poor devils that lives in them shacks out yonder ain't got enough to eat the way it is!" Timmons protested. "And I don't work so good if I don't get my belly filled up regular."

"When the food reaches here, there will be enough for you to share with the *poblachos,* if you wish," O'Riley said.

"You still ain't told me when you aim to come back," Timmons reminded him. "If it's real soon, I'll likely need to get busy stamping out that new batch of rounds you said you'd be wanting."

"When I return will depend on many things," O'Riley replied. "And in any case, it is not of your concern. Do your work as you always do. When we need the rounds I will expect you to have them ready."

Longarm broke in to protest. "You're saying I got to wait here all chained up and not know when I'll be getting free? Now, that ain't—"

"*Callate!*" O'Riley snapped. "Be quiet!" When Longarm said nothing, he went on. "I will give you advice that will save you much trouble. Do not make the mistake of trying to escape. If you are no threat to me, I might think of keeping you here. Perhaps I would even pay you if I give you employment. But this is not the time for talk. I have more important business that I must care for. Do not cause any trouble for Timmons here. If you do, you will be very regretful."

While Longarm was still trying to decide on a reply, Umberto returned. He was carrying Longarm's Winchester and gunbelt. He dropped them at Timmons's feet and turned to O'Riley, cocking his head in an unspoken question.

"*Dejamos aqui, con Timmons,*" O'Riley told him. "*Ahorita, vaminos. Sobre el rancho hay cosas muy importantas que attendemos.*"

Without looking at Longarm and Timmons again, O'Riley reined his horse around and toed the animal ahead. Umberto hurried to follow him. Longarm and Timmons watched them as they headed back to the rising ground and vanished around the curving trail, the burros following.

"How come you didn't tell him who I was, Timmons?" Longarm asked as they turned away from watching the departing procession. When Timmons shrugged, Longarm went on. "Looks like I owe you."

"Damned if I know," the tall lanky man replied. "It just didn't seem like to me that it'd be the right thing to do."

"Well, now," Longarm said, "I don't mind telling you, there were times while you two were palavering that I got a mite upset. I kept looking for you to tell him I was a lawman from the States. If you'd done that, I got a notion that he'd've plugged me right then and there. How come you didn't say anything?"

"To tell you the honest truth, I just plain don't know," Timmons answered. "But maybe it was because you treated me decenter than any lawman I ever got arrested by."

"It's been such a long time since I hauled you in that I'd sorta forgot who you was when I saw you," Longarm as he began to loosen the rope from around his neck. "It took a minute or two for me to come up with your name and remember why I had to haul you in to jail."

"Hell, I been in twenty more jails since then," Timmons said. "Not because I done something really bad, but mainly on account of it's still easier to steal than it is to work."

"Well, I can't say as I'd agree with you on that, seeing as we're on different sides of the law. But that ain't here nor there. It'd look to me like you stuck your head into a mess of trouble. That O'Riley fellow's going to be madder'n a wet hen if he finds out you was trying to help me."

"Except that I don't aim to be here when he comes back. I ain't had no place to belly up to the bar or set down at a regular table and stow away a good meal for a pretty good while. Lately I been figuring that it's time I pulled up stakes and got back across the border."

"How'd you come to tie in with that Don Carlos O'Riley fellow?"

"All I can say, it was one of them things that just happens," Timmons replied. "I had to dodge across the Rio Grande into Mexico to get away from the law, and I didn't know the ropes down here from Adam's off-ox. I reckon you'll remember that I was blacksmithing before I got tied up with that safecracking outfit up in Laramie?"

"Sure," Longarm replied. "And as I recall, you busted outa jail before you was due to stand trial."

"That wasn't such a much of a job." Timmons grinned. "But after I'd broke out I knew I'd be in a worse fix than ever if the law caught up with me again. To cut a long story short, I drifted down here south of the Rio Grande, and I knew I'd be in real trouble if I got caught. Then I run into Don Carlos and found out he was looking for a good metalworking man, so I asked for the job and got it."

"And you been here ever since?"

"That's right. I bossed the crew that put up these buildings here, and after they was up Don Carlos propositioned me to stay on and run the job I'm doing now."

"I don't reckon you'd mind telling me just what it is you do for him," Longarm said. He was sure he already knew the kind of work Timmons was doing and hoped he'd get an honest answer.

"I got a notion you already know that, Longarm."

"Maybe I do and maybe I don't. But even if I do, I'd like to hear you tell me."

Timmons did not reply for several moments. At last he said, "I stamp rounds the size of a twenty-dollar gold piece outa brass plate. Made the dies myself, and it taken me a long time to do the engraving so's the rounds look just like a double eagle. After they get dipped in melted

106

gold and the gold sets up, a man'd be pretty hard put to tell what they really are. Why, you got to look close at 'em to see they ain't real double eagles that's come outa the U.S. Mint."

Longarm nodded. "I figured that's what it was, because I was sent down here to stop just exactly what you're doing."

"Sure. I tumbled to that right off, when I seen you. But how'd Don Carlos managed to get hold of you, Longarm?"

"He surprised me on the trail. But you'd have to say I bamboozled him. It appears that he ain't figured out yet I'm a U.S. lawman," Longarm replied. "And I'm betting that the burros he's leading back to his ranch are loaded up with a batch of those faked gold pieces you've made up."

"You'd win your bet, all right," Timmons said. "He comes here regular to haul away all the ones I've made up."

Longarm went on. "Unless I'm wrong, there's somebody down in Monterrey waiting for 'em. That's the only thing I could figure out that'd put him in such an all-fired rush."

"I can't tell you a thing about where he goes or what he does. He don't hardly talk at all while he's here. Just between me and you, he's been taking out a good load of gold-coated brass every time he comes here," Timmons said. "But you figure he don't know why you're here?"

Longarm shook his head. "He ain't said a lot yet, but that don't make much never-mind. When I stopped at Monterrey on my way here, I had a little brush with the *rurales,* and they went through a lot of papers I was carrying. What was in those papers is enough to start everybody in O'Riley's bunch of crooks trying to

107

find me. You know what they say about dead men not telling any tales."

"Well, I still don't understand much yet about where all them fake double eagles is going to," Timmons said. "But that Don Carlos is about the most closed-mouthed man I ever run into. He'll come pick up a batch of them counterfeits and ride away with his little pack train, and all the time he's here he don't say a dozen words."

"You just been sticking too close to here to find out much of anything," Longarm said. "He's got himself a bank now, down in Monterrey. And the U.S. Mint's short on gold a lot of the time, so the Treasury's been buying them counterfeited double eagles from his bank and some other banks down here. Then when they finally tumbled to what Don Carlos was doing, they had me sent down here to stop him stealing from Uncle Sam."

"Well, I'll be damned!" Timmons exclaimed. "Why, he's about as bold as the brass is in them fake double eagles!"

"Sure," Longarm said. "And if you're wanting to get away from here, you might as well ride along with me when I head back to his ranch, because I got to dog after him till I get all the evidence I need to arrest him."

"You've got yourself a deal," Timmons agreed. "There's a few things I'd reckon you'd want to do before we head out, like getting them double eagle molds, but it won't take that much time to handle 'em."

"We'll do what we got to," Longarm said. "And soon as we finish here, we'll cut a shuck back to the O'Riley ranch. If I can catch Don Carlos before he leaves for Monterrey, it'll sure make my job easier."

Chapter 10

"I reckon you've got the right idea about taking these molds with us," Timmons told Longarm as he lifted a square thick piece of metal from a cabinet beside the workbench and laid it on the bench. "If they stay here Don Carlos could find somebody else to do my job and he'd keep right on using 'em."

"It's not just a notion that's got into me," Longarm said. "Part of what I got to do on this case I'm working down here is dig up all of the counterfeiting gear I can get my hands on, molds and all like that, and take it back with me."

"Wouldn't it be easier just to break up the molds here, so they couldn't be used again?"

"Oh, sure. That's what I tried to tell my chief before I set out. But it seems like the Secret Service back in Washington figures they can get some good out of studying 'em over because there might be some things that'd help them to track down other counterfeit artists."

"Well, that's one sure way to keep Don Carlos from using the molds anymore," Timmons said. "And it looks like to me that they oughta be about all you need. But to tell you the truth, I sorta hate to see 'em go. I sure did put in a lot of time and work engraving 'em."

Timmons had taken a second mold from the cabinet while Longarm was talking. He laid it beside the first one, and was moving to take out another when Longarm stretched a hand out to stop him.

"Maybe you better tell me how this kind of work's done. From what I managed to pick up before I left, there ain't any two counterfeiters that works the same way," Longarm said. "Because it's likely I'll have to do some court testifying about it. Generally, the Secret Service takes all the counterfeiting cases. The only other one I ever worked was to round up a gang that was printing fake dollar bills, and that was quite a while ago."

"Printing paper money's easy when you put it up alongside copying coins," Timmons assured him. "Pouring in the melted gold's a miserable job, and a man that's doing it has got to work real fast. Priming the molds has got to be done awful quick. In a regular government mint they stamp out the coins in big presses, but that takes all sorts of machinery. Pouring's a harder way. It's when you pour one batch at a time that you got to be real careful."

"Go ahead, I'm listening," Longarm told him.

"There's not all that much to it," Timmons went on. "Just take a look at the way these molds are made and you'll see. You got to remember that they're carved backwards so the fake double eagles are right side up. All these little troughs connect them. You put a dabble of beeswax on each side of your round brass blank so as to hold them in the middle of the mold and lay a blank in every dent."

"You mean that's all there is to it?"

"Oh, there's a little bit more. After you clamp the molds together you got to bury 'em in the coals set up on edge. When they get good and hot, you pour in the melted gold and it runs down and burns up the wax. When the wax runs out, the hot gold fills all the openings. After you let the molds cool and open them up, what you've got left is a little layer of gold over a brass slug."

When Timmons stopped to take a fresh breath, Longarm asked, "Don't the blanks sorta shift around in the holes when you set them molds up that way?"

"A few of them might move a little bit, but if you know your business and handle the molds right when you're setting them up, there won't be more than three or four that gets spoiled," Timmons replied. "And they don't go to waste. You just melt the gold off of the brass blanks and use them in your next run."

"So when you finish what you call a run, you got a batch of what'll pass for real American double eagles?" Longarm asked.

"That's the size of it," Timmons agreed. "The only trick is knowing when everything's ready. Once you've got that down pat, you're bound to do a good job."

Shaking his head, Longarm said, "Well, it sure ain't a job I'd go looking for. How long did it take you to learn all that rigamarole?"

Timmons was silent for a moment, a thoughtful frown puckering up his face. Then he said, "I was just about twelve years old when my daddy put me to apprentice with a good goldsmith. Then it was four or five years before I learned all the tricks of the trade. I stayed on for a while after that. Then I got off on a sidetrack. One thing led to another till I wound up on the wrong side of the law. But you'd know all about that, Longarm, seeing it was you that arrested me."

"Sure. But that was a while back, and I don't suppose I've thought much about it until I seen you when Don Carlos brought me here. You've changed a mite, but generally I don't forget somebody I've arrested."

"I hope you're not figuring on arresting me again?"

"Well, I try not to lie to anybody when I can tell the truth just as easy, but I got to go by the rules and the law," Longarm said. His voice was thoughtful and he spoke a bit more deliberately than usual. "I ain't inclined to arrest you because you're giving me a hand on this case."

"I'm glad to hear you say that," Timmons said.

"I ain't quite finished," Longarm warned him. "The thing is, you been helping Don Carlos O'Riley rob the U.S. Mint, even if you're doing it down here in Mexico."

"It wasn't a thing I wanted to do."

"Maybe not, except the fact is, you done it."

"But if I help you, I ought not to be in trouble!" Timmons protested.

"That's what I'm getting around to," Longarm said. "Now, as long as we're in Mexico, my badge ain't much good. If I want my arrest to stick, I got to haul you back across the Rio Grande to make everything legal, but don't make no mistake about it, that's what I aim to do."

"Then I guess I'll stand trial and go to jail again?"

"Oh, you'll likely get put up in front of a judge," Longarm agreed. "But I got a hunch you'll get off scot-free when your trial come up, because I'd stand up in court and tell the judge that you gave me a hand."

"It makes me feel better to hear you come right out and say that," Timmons told Longarm.

"Sure," Longarm said. "You know, law or no law, if I had a stick or two of dynamite, I'd blow up this layout, but there ain't no place short of Monterrey where I could get any."

"You're talking the way I did a while back," Timmons said. His voice was subdued. "There was a time right after I first started working for Don Carlos when he treated me like he does his *peones*, and that made me real mad."

"I reckon I can understand that," Longarm told him. "He don't appear to me like he's a man that's easy to get along with."

"You can say that two or three times in a row and stack it up," Timmons said. "Why, he pushed me so hard I even got some sticks of dynamite when he sent me down to Monterrey one day, I was that ready to blow up this place."

"Except you never got around to doing it. I can see that."

"No, but I've still got the dynamite tucked away, even if I don't ever expect to use it."

"Have you, now?" Longarm said. "You don't reckon it's gone bad, do you?"

"I couldn't say, because I haven't had any reason to look at it for a long time," Timmons answered. "I buried it over in that corner yonder, so Don Carlos wouldn't be likely to stumble onto it."

"Well, if I can get Don Carlos across the Rio Grande, you won't have much to stay here for," Longarm said. "But right this minute, we got to stop palavering and get moving towards that ranch, or I'll miss grabbing Don Carlos."

"You're going to arrest him, I guess?" Timmons said, as they began tucking the coin molds and the bag of brass rounds into Longarm's saddlebags.

"I sure aim to, even if my badge ain't worth much on this side of the border."

"Count on me to help you all I can," Timmons volunteered. "I know you've got to arrest me and take me back with you, and I don't object to that any longer. But I figure anything I do might make a judge go easier on me if I stand up on your side."

"It likely will," Longarm agreed. "But I been trying for quite a while to figure out how we're going to get back to the ranch with just that one horse I was riding. I reckon it's lucky he left it, but it sure ain't up to carrying double, not with all them molds and other stuff that'll go into my saddlebags."

"Don't worry about that," Timmons said. "The villagers always have a couple of horses straying around, and I've borrowed one now and again when I had to hurry down to Don Carlos's ranch with a bag of fake money."

"You might as well carry your gear outside and start chasing one of 'em down then," Longarm suggested. "I'll finish up here and we'll move on out."

As soon as Timmons started toward the nearest of the little shacks, Longarm picked up a shovel that was lying beside the heap of dead coals and went to the corner which Timmons had indicated as the location of the buried dynamite. He used the shovel carefully, taking off a thin layer of dirt each time he dug into the hard-crusted earthen floor.

"Just you take it easy, old son," Longarm muttered as he worked. "Remember what you learned about this stuff when you was a young kid working for that canal gang back home. Dynamite's tricky when it's fresh, and it's a good sight trickier when it starts getting older. Mind your P's and Q's now, and get these here dynamite sticks free without blowing yourself to kingdom come."

When he felt the edge of the shovel meet a sudden resistance, he laid the shovel aside and hunkered down beside the small excavation. Now Longarm used only his hands to scrape away the loosened earth until he'd uncovered a cloth-wrapped bundle. Its elongated shape told him he'd found what he was looking for, and as he scraped away the dirt around its edges he could feel the coil of fuse that Timmons had buried with the dynamite.

"Looks like you're home free," Longarm told himself as he carried the bundle to the center of the shed. "All you got to do from here on in is put everything together."

When he reached the center of the building Longarm lowered his bundle to the ground. Then, handling it very gently indeed, he unwrapped the cloth that covered the explosive sticks. There were five of them, as well as a small string of crimped copper detonators. Spreading the cloth on the ground beside him, Longarm placed the dynamite sticks in its center and gingerly inserted one of the detonators in each stick's end. The explosive mixture that filled the paper tubes had softened with time, and the detonators slid in easily.

Now Longarm picked up the coil of fuse and unrolled it, heading for the door of the shed. He stopped just inside the door and let two or three more loops drop off the coil. Taking out his pocketknife, he stooped and cut the fuse. There was a sizeable amount of fuse remaining, and he studied the back and side walls of the big metal structure for a moment.

"Five sticks of dynamite," he said under his breath. "And there's enough fuse to reach them two back corners with. If you're going to do a job, old son, remember what granddad used to say back in West Virginia. 'Do it right

the first time, then you won't have to do it twice.'
Except that when you're doing a job like this there's
only one time."

As Longarm talked, he was cutting from the coil more
lengths of fuse. Placing the fuse ends he'd cut on the
ground by the door, he ran lengths of fuse to each back
corner of the building.

Picking up his original charge, he carefully detached
two of the five sticks of dynamite. These he took to the
rear of the room and attached to the fuse ends he'd left
at the corners. Longarm wiped his hands on the ground,
then rubbed them together for a moment to remove the
sticky liquid that had oozed from the dynamite sticks.
Then he returned to the spot where he'd left the three
sticks of dynamite, and working very gingerly, replaced
their detonators.

He stepped back, and was surveying his work when
the thudding of hoofbeats sounded outside. He moved
quickly to the door and went outside. Timmons was just
reining in when Longarm emerged. The horse Timmons
had found was swaybacked and its ribs ran in ridges under
its frowsty coat.

"I won't guarantee how good this nag is, but it's the
only one I could spook up," he said.

"You know, I figured the livery horse I hired down in
Monterrey was a pretty sorry nag, but it looks like this
one's got mine beat for ugly," Longarm remarked.

"It was the only one I could catch up to," Timmons
replied. "But I figure it'll hold up till we get to Monterrey.
You ready to ride out now?"

"Ready as I'll ever be," Longarm replied. "My saddlebags are just inside the door. I'll step back and pick 'em
up, then we'll be ready to take out."

"Heading for Monterrey?" Timmons asked.

"I figure we'd best stop at Don Carlos's ranch house. I know he ain't likely to be there, but maybe Miz O'Riley can tell us where we oughta start looking for him."

Longarm was taking a match from his pocket as he turned to enter the building. He scraped his thumbnail across the match head as he picked up the free ends of the fuses he'd laid so carefully and touched the match's flaring flame to the ends. Spurts of dancing sparks shot from them as Longarm let the fuses fall to the floor. He grabbed his saddlebags and stepped up to his horse, tossed the saddlebags in place, and swung into the saddle.

"Let's don't waste no time getting outa here," he said to Timmons, reining his horse around as he dug his boot toe into its ribs and prodded it to a quick walk. "The more ground we put between us and this place, the better I'm going to like it."

Timmons turned his horse and drummed his boot heels on its barrel to catch up with Longarm. "What's your all-fired hurry?" he called. "We'll give these sorry nags the heaves if we try to keep 'em going this fast!"

Longarm nodded, but said nothing. Timmons spurred his mount abreast and swiveled in his saddle as he called, "What the hell's got into you, Longarm? There ain't no call to—"

Whatever Timmons intended to say was drowned out by the dull rolling roar of the dynamite blast. Both he and Longarm twisted in their saddles as they reined in to look back.

They saw the building they'd just left hanging in mid-air, a wide gap of smoke-blotted daylight between it and the ground. The next two explosions sounded almost as one. They were not as loud as the first one had been, but the shock as the last two sticks of dynamite detonated shook the suspended building and set its walls dancing.

117

Only a few seconds passed before the walls came apart, their sheets of crumpling metal flopping and twisting as they dropped back to earth. At the same time the roof was separating into its own individual tin sheets. Some flipped, some wobbled as they hung in midair for a few fleeting seconds before crashing as they plummeted to the ground on the bent quivering remnants of the walls.

Smoke, the greenish-yellow cloud created by the dynamite began surging up and rolling across the surface of the ground where the building had stood. For a moment the lower layer of deep yellow smoke clouds roiled as they rose. Then they began to lift and to dissipate. Between the heavier wisps of rising smoke Longarm and Timmons could now see a few of the villagers running toward the spot where the building had stood.

"I'd guess them poor devils figures the end of the world's come," Timmons said. "I reckon they'll get over it, though."

"Sure they will," Longarm agreed. "But it'd sure lift Don Carlos O'Riley's hackles more'n a little bit if he was here right now watching this."

"What do you reckon he'll do when he finds out?"

"Why, the way I look at it, there ain't much he can do," Longarm replied. He flicked his eyes across the flattened expanse where the ruins of the building lay and added, "Anyways, he ain't likely to get much of a chance to look at it. We'll head for his ranch house now. If he's there, the first thing I aim to do is arrest him."

"I thought you told me your badge ain't any good here in Mexico," Timmons said.

"It ain't," Longarm said. "And it's likely Don Carlos knows that's the way of it. But if I can't persuade him with my badge, I'll likely be able to with my Colt."

"Figuring you'll take him back across the Rio Grande, are you?" Timmons asked.

"Sure. It's United States money he's been counterfeiting. And you can't bring a man to trial in Mexico for something he's done to break the law of the United States."

"Hell's bells, Longarm! Don Carlos has got more friends in Monterrey than you can shake a stick at. And in Mexico City too." Timmons snorted. "But it's your case, and I guess you can say I'm your prisoner too."

"I'm sorta sorry it's got to be that way," Longarm said. "And you're right about being my prisoner, but I don't imagine I'm going to have to drag you back across the Rio Grande."

"This time you're the one that's right," Timmons agreed. "I sure don't aim to give you any trouble, Longarm. And if you need it, I'll give you whatever help I can."

"Let's leave it at that and see what happens." Longarm suggested. "We'll see what's what when we get to the ranch house. If Don Carlos is there, I'll arrest him fast. If he ain't, we'll go on to Monterrey."

Darkness had fallen by the time their tiring horses brought Longarm and Timmons to the Rancho Miraflores. They could see a few lighted windows in the sprawling main house as well as in the small huts of the servants' quarters that dotted the area where the outbuildings of the *rancho* were located.

"Well, now that we've got here, we ain't going to have to guess about what to do," Longarm said. "Now, I'm going to have to do something that I don't like to, but I got to do it because it's my duty."

"I won't have to guess much to figure it out," Timmons told him. "You're going to handcuff me."

"That's right. And I'll take your word that you won't try to make a getaway or mix up in any sorta fracas I might run into. Even if it ain't real likely that Don Carlos is here, I got to stop and make sure."

"I understand all that," Timmons replied. "You've got my word that I'm on your side now, and I aim to keep it that way."

They rode in silence up to the door of the imposing ranch building and reined in. Longarm fumbled his handcuffs out of his saddlebag and toed his horse up close enough to Timmons's to fit the shackles around his companion's wrists.

"Should Don Carlos be here, it'll look better if you got these on," he said. "Sorta gives him the idea that you and me ain't in cahoots, and it might just save trouble."

"Sure," Timmons agreed. "Having those things on won't bother me a bit."

"Now, just sit quiet," Longarm said as he dismounted. "It won't take me more'n two minutes to find out what's what and how much trouble we'll be running into."

Chapter 11

Swinging out of his saddle, Longarm stepped up to the *hacienda*'s imposing front door and rapped. He'd waited only a moment or two before the door swung open to reveal a man holding a lighted lantern.

"*Bienvenido, señor,*" he said as he lifted the lantern to get a better look at Longarm. "*Cualquier es que quiere?*"

"I reckon you understand English?" Longarm said.

"A leetle beet. You weesh what?"

"If Don Carlos O'Riley's here, it's him I'm looking for," Longarm replied. "If he ain't, I don't reckon it's too late in the day to talk with Miz O'Riley."

Before the house servant could reply, Adelita O'Riley appeared at the door. She said, "It is not too late, Señor Long. Please come in." As Longarm stepped past the servant and entered the house, she went on. "But if you wish to speak with my husband, he is already on his way to Monterrey."

"I sorta figured he might've left, but I wanted to make sure," Longarm told her. "Likely I can find him at his bank, so I won't bother you no more. I'll just ride on down there."

"Are you in so great a hurry that you cannot stop for a short while to rest? And perhaps take a bit of refreshment? Have you yet had an evening meal?"

"Why, I've had saddle rations, ma'am. They were plenty good enough, and there's enough left to tide me over. But I ain't planning on stopping very long here since Don Carlos ain't at home. Besides that, I got somebody with me I'm a U.S. marshal, ma'am."

"Then the man on the horse out there is a prisoner?" she said. "I hope you have not found it necessary to arrest one of our people from the *rancho*."

"Not unless you'd say that big shed up in the hills is part of your ranch, ma'am. And I don't know whether you'd call the man I got with me a ranch hand, but you'd likely know about him, and maybe even why I had to arrest him. His name's Timmons, and if you don't know it, he's got himself into trouble with the law in the United States."

"I have heard Carlos mention his name. I also know of the place where he was working, of course, but of what he was doing, or what he has done to break your country's law, I know nothing," Adelita replied. After a moment of hesitation she added, "You must understand that Carlos does not discuss all his business affairs with me."

"From what I've noticed, that's the way it is in a lot of families in your country," Longarm said. "I've run into it on cases I've worked down here before. Now, I don't want to turn down your kind invite, but it's best that I do."

Adelita said quickly, "If you will excuse me for insisting, Marshal Long, it would please me greatly if you could stop for even a short time. It is very late, and the road to Monterrey is not an easy one, especially in the darkness. But there are some matters I would like to discuss with you, if you are not in too great a hurry."

Longarm hesitated for only a moment before replying, "Well, I'd like to oblige you, ma'am, but I got to keep my eye on that fellow outside. And I sure can't imagine what them matters might be you want to talk about. Maybe if you were to give me some sorta hint . . ."

Adelita shook her head. "Such a thing I cannot yet do. There is too great a risk that one of the servants might overhear us talking. I would not wish that to happen."

"Well, the way you put it sure makes it sound like it's important," Longarm said. "And I'd like to oblige you, but my main business right now is to get that prisoner out there down to Monterrey safe and sound."

"I'm sure that you can trust Tomas—he is our house servant—to guard your prisoner carefully," she said. "I will caution him to be careful, if you wish to hear what I have to say. And if you should . . ." Adelita stopped short, but after a moment of silence went on. "I am keeping you from your meal. And I am sure your prisoner must be as hungry as you are."

"Likely he is," Longarm agreed.

"Then I will have Tomas give him food in the servants' quarters," Adelita said. "And you will be served in our family dining room. Come, let us go there, and while you are eating, we can talk."

"Well, I sure ain't going to turn down your kind invite," Longarm told her. "A hot cup of coffee'd go down real fine right now. And I got to admit, I'm a mite curious to find out what it is you're so interested in talking about."

As Adelita led Longarm to the small dining room he'd seen on his earlier stop at the *rancho* she assured him,

"Coffee is always ready here. And when you are refreshed it will take but little time to satisfy your curiosity. But if you are going to Monterrey, you will need more than coffee to sustain you."

"Why, I've missed meals before. Putting off another one ain't such a much."

"Since you'll be returning on the road which you took here from Monterrey, you're certainly aware that you are beginning a long ride. I'm sure you discovered that there is no store along it where you can buy food on the way there. The only store is the one you must've passed near the trail fork, but it does not sell any kind of food."

"Oh, I ain't counting on that place, ma'am. I already found out it ain't a grocery store when I stopped at it on the way here to your ranch," Longarm said. "The fellow that runs it gave me a bite or two, but it came out of his own kitchen."

Adelita's voice was very firm. "Then I will insist on you stopping here long enough for my cook to prepare supper for you and your companion. This can be done quickly. While you eat, I will also have the cook provide a packet that you can carry with you. I will tell her to be sure there is enough to keep both you and your prisoner from being hungry on your way to Monterrey."

"Now, I wasn't expecting to put you to all that kind of trouble, ma'am."

"It is no trouble," she assured him.

"Well, when push comes to shove, that is a sorta long ride to take when a man's stomach's griping," Longarm said. "So if it ain't going to be too troublesome, I'll just take your kind invite. Me and Timmons was in such a hurry to get away from that place where he's been working that we didn't even try to rustle up any grub before we left."

"Providing two food packets is a small matter," Adelita said as she stood up. "Please excuse me for leaving for a short time. I must give the necessary orders. One of the kitchen maids will bring your food soon, but do not wait for me to return before you begin your meal."

A few moments after Adelita had gone a woman servant brought in a tray holding a napkin-covered plate and saucer in addition to a small steaming coffeepot and cup. She placed the tray on the table and gestured for Longarm to sit down, then left the room.

When Longarm settled himself at the table and removed the napkin covering the plate, he discovered that it held a sizeable piece of steak and a dollop of rice, while on the saucer there was a small stack of steaming-hot *tortillas*. The sight and aroma of the food stirred Longarm's appetite. He began eating, and had finished his impromptu meal when Adelita returned.

During her absence she had changed into another robe, a creation of shimmering pink silk with a high lace neck that cradled her chin. As it dropped from her shoulders it clung to her body and emphasized her generous breasts and slim waist. She settled into a chair across the table from him.

"Although you did little more than mention my husband," she said, "I take it you found him? I hope you also had a satisfactory conversation?"

"You might say we sorta got acquainted," Longarm replied. "And I ain't going to go much beyond that, because as you've said, he never said much to you about what he was doing up in the hills."

"This is true," Adelita agreed.

"So I don't reckon you'd know a lot about that big bank he's got down in Monterrey?"

"I have visited the bank only once," she admitted. "It was at a time when there were important people from the capital who had come to Monterrey to discuss business with Carlos, and he wished to entertain them at a banquet."

"Well, now, that's right interesting," Longarm commented. "I just wonder if you recall any of their names."

"There were so many people there that I can remember only a few," she said. "But why do you ask?"

"Oh, I got some other folks besides your husband I need to talk to before I can close my case. I just figured it'd be handy if I could get him to introduce me around, should I need help."

Adelita shook her head. "That is a matter of which Carlos himself must be the judge."

"Then I'll just wait till I get to Monterrey and do my own asking," Longarm told her. He pushed his chair away from the table and stood up. "Now, when I first came in, I recall you saying that you had something you want to talk about with me. Can we sit down and have a little chat now, while my prisoner finishes eating?"

"Of course," Adelita agreed. "We can talk here or we can go into my *salon*. Perhaps that would be the best thing to do. The servants will be clearing the table here. In the *salon* we will be able to talk without interruption."

Adelita led Longarm down a wide hall until they reached a doorway. She opened the door and gestured for Longarm to follow her down another corridor. He did so, his boot heels sinking so deeply into the deep velvet-like carpeting that he almost lost his balance. Adelita stopped in front of another doorway, opened the door, and gestured for Longarm to enter. Following him inside, she closed the door.

Longarm glanced around the room he'd gone into. It was small in comparison to most of the rooms he'd seen in the sprawling ranch house, and was carpeted so luxuriously that his boot heels sank deeply into the lush pile of the rug. If there were windows in the room, they were hidden by the light-hued shimmering silken draperies that covered the walls and swept in billowing arcs from the ceiling.

The room's furnishings were sparse but luxurious. A wide divan upholstered in velvet dominated the room, spanning most of one wall. A small elaborately carved desk stood on the opposite wall, a chair drawn up to it, and a lamp glowed on its top, lighting the room with a warm glow. Two more velvet-upholstered chairs standing near the desk completed its furnishings.

"None of the house servants would dare to disturb me when I am in here," Adelita said as she closed the door and turned to face Longarm. "Even Carlos would think twice before intruding."

"It's a right pretty room," Longarm told her. "I reckon everybody oughta have a place where they can be by themselves and do some private thinking."

"I'm glad you understand," Adelita said, gesturing toward the divan. As they settled down on it she went on. "Now, let us sit and talk for a moment. Since you stopped here I have been doing much thinking, and I have a certain request to make."

"You go right ahead and make it then. I'll listen real careful," Longarm assured her.

"First, I must tell you that the *rancho* here was my dowry when Carlos and I were married. It was proper for him to take it as his own, but now I find that I am shut out from any of its operation. My husband is no longer the man he was when we were first married."

"Well, I'm sorry to hear you say that, but I got to tell you that I ain't much of a one to mix in with family problems," Longarm said.

"I am not asking that you do so. But Carlos has too many other affairs now to occupy him and take his attention away from me. And I fear that the course he is following will bring him much trouble. At this moment he has some affair going on of which I know nothing."

"You mean he's got some other woman on his string?"

Adelita shook her head. "Another woman would be nothing new. Husbands here are not known for being faithful. No, Marshal Long. It is something to do with money, much money. Dishonest money as well."

"Now from what I understand, that ain't too unusual down here in Mexico," Longarm said. "Ain't it sorta the custom of the country?"

"There is much of dishonesty," Adelita admitted. "But to you I will speak the truth. I do not regret Carlos's seeking out other women, for it leaves me free to find my satisfaction with other men. I do not turn to the ranch hands, as others in my position do. But that is something aside from what is my great concern at the moment. It is money that I speak of."

Adelita's confessions were only mildly surprising to Longarm. He had bedded with enough women to have learned that many of them found more satisfaction with men other than their husbands. Her mention of money was another matter, for he realized at once that it could somehow involve the gold swindle which he'd been sent to investigate.

"Well, ma'am, I guess everybody's interested in money," Longarm said. "Gold money's what's brought me here to Mexico, and I'd sure be right interested in hearing what you got to say about it."

"For some reason which I do not understand, Carlos has taken all the gold coins from the household funds we keep on hand here. This was the money we need to buy cattle-breeding stock and to pay our servants and the ranch hands and the merchants with whom we deal in Monterrey," she said. "Only a short time ago I discovered that all the gold was gone."

"I reckon you asked him about it?"

"He was not here for me to ask. He was in Monterrey, at the new bank which he had just opened."

"Then I'd imagine you asked him when he got home?"

"Of certainty," Adelita said. "At first Carlos said only that he was responsible for our household funds. Then when I persisted with my questions, he flew into a rage. He called me vile names. He grasped my shoulders and began to shake me."

As she spoke, Adelita stood up and stepped in front of him. She lifted her hands to unbutton the neck of her gown and pulled it open to bare her throat and shoulders. Though the marks were fading, against her clear white skin Longarm saw the purpling blotches of bruises and the small circles where the tips of clawing fingers had grasped her.

"Well, I got to agree that ain't a real pretty sight," he said. "But what happened after that?"

"Carlos left for Monterrey at once," Adelita answered. "When he returned, the day before you stopped here, he avoided me for the few hours he stayed. As soon as he could summon the servants required, and have them make ready the pack animals, he left to go to Las Cumbres. Then you came looking for him. The rest you know."

"And it ain't a real pretty story, I got to agree," Longarm said. "But I can't figure out why you told me all of what you did. Sure, I got a law man's badge, but it don't give me no right to step into a family fuss."

Adelita was silent for a moment. Then she said, "I do not myself know why I spoke so freely. Perhaps it was only that I had no one else to tell. Perhaps it was to anger you with Carlos so that you would . . ." She stopped short and shook her head. "No. I would have brought you here no matter what had happened between me and Carlos. And I am sure you know why I did. When I see a man I desire. I wish him also to desire me."

"Well, I got to admit you speak right out," Longarm told her. He began unbuckling his gunbelt. "And I'd have to be a lot less of a man if I didn't do what you're hinting at."

Longarm had the gunbelt off by the time he'd finished speaking. He stooped to place it on the floor beside the divan, and as he straightened up Adelita stepped closer to him. She had begun to free the buttons remaining on her dress. Longarm extended his hand to help her. Adelita left it to him to undo the remaining buttons and started unbuckling the belt of his trousers.

Longarm pulled Adelita's gown off her shoulders at almost the same time that she began to work his trousers down to his thighs. She released him long enough to let her dress fall in a heap, revealing that she wore nothing beneath it. Longarm used the moment to lever out of his boots, and Adelita resumed pushing his trousers down until they were heaped around his feet.

Now the bulge of his erection was stretching Longarm's underwear. He waited until Adelita interrupted her finger-caresses and used the moment to finish removing her dress.

Longarm made short work of ridding himself of his last garment. Wasting no time, Adelita locked her hands behind Longarm's shoulders and pulled him with her as she took the small backward step that allowed her to sink to the divan. For a moment they squirmed and turned, Adelita's hand groping between their bodies for a moment to place his erection.

"Now!" she said urgently. "Drive now!"

Longarm was more than ready. He delivered the lusty thrust she'd called for and buried himself completely.

Adelita gasped. Her cry could have been a small scream or a sob of satisfaction at his penetration. She rotated her hips, slowly at first, then rapidly. Her eyes closed, and she locked her legs across his back in an effort to bring him into her even more deeply.

Longarm remained motionless for a moment, waiting for Adelita to release his hips. After she'd squirmed and sighed for several moments he felt the grip of her tensed cradling thighs relax. Then he began thrusting.

He did not hurry, but went into her warm yielding softness with slow measured strokes, almost withdrawing completely and holding himself motionless above her for a moment before starting to repeat his deep penetrations. When small tremors began to ripple through Adelita's soft body, Longarm stopped his steady rhythmic stroking. Now he held himself fully in her until her shivers stopped. Then he began thrusting once more.

For several minutes after Longarm resumed his steadily paced drives, Adelita responded only languidly. Then, as though she was responding to some sudden shock, she began jerking her hips wildly, rotating them as she moved. Longarm did not try to match her rhythm. He waited until her body began trembling and her soft sighs of pleasure

131

grew louder, small half-smothered screams that escaped her lips more often.

Longarm started thrusting then, driving with increasing force and holding himself pressed to her while the undulations of her hips became a constant twisting rocking. When her cries became more intense and the rhythm of her moving hips grew spastic and rapid, he speeded his own rhythm and drove with greater force.

Adelita suddenly loosed an explosive scream and her body tensed as her hips rolled in a frantic frenzy. She bucked and squirmed and Longarm pounded with a final penetration, deeper than any before it. He held himself to her, pressing hard, while her hips gyrated wildly and a steady babble of estatic shouts burst from her lips.

Adelita's screams filled the room for several moments, and when they began to subside Longarm drove fast and hard in deep quick thrusts until he reached his own climax. He held himself pressed to Adelita while he jetted, and while her final moments of fulfillment grew slower until she was quiet, except for an occasional spastic shudder. When Longarm felt her subsiding, he let himself relax and lay sprawled on her soft body, totally satisfied and spent.

Chapter 12

"You are indeed a powerful lover," Adelita said. She spoke in a half whisper and her voice carried the purring tone of satisfaction. She and Longarm were lying side by side, pressed close together, both motionless.

"Well, I ain't one to pass judgment on myself," Longarm told her. "But if I pleasured you good, I got to say that you sure done the same by me."

"Then we have pleased one another. If you will stay the night with me, we can enjoy more pleasure."

"I reckon the best thing I can say is yes," he answered. "And I feel about like you do. I can sure stand another go or two with you."

"I'm sure you know that I will not leave you," Adelita promised. "You are welcome to stay as long as you wish."

"I can't stay much past daylight, but I'd a heap rather start riding when I can see the road and make good time as to plug along slow in the dark."

"Darkness is for lovers, not for riding," Adelita said. Her hands were moving over Longarm's crotch now and he was responding to their soft caresses. "And if I keep the curtains drawn we can stay in darkness as long as you wish."

"And that'd be quite a while, if I could stay. But I got my job to finish, which means hauling that fellow back to Monterrey soon as I can. I don't reckon I got to worry none about him tonight, seeing as your man's keeping tabs on him."

"Thomas always obeys my orders, so you have no need to worry about your prisoner," Adelita assured him. As she spoke her hand was cradling Longarm's groin. Then her fingers closed to clasp him in a soft caress. After a moment of silence she went on. "Ah, my fingers are telling me that you are almost ready to share our pleasures once more. And now that all has been settled, we will have the rest of the night together."

"If you just keep on doing what you're doing now, I sure won't keep you waiting," Longarm said. "And I don't mind telling you, I'm ready as you are to start from scratch again."

"Damn it, Longarm, you still ain't told me what you're aiming to do with me after we get to Monterry," Timmons complained. "I got a right to know, after all the help I've been to you. Making me drag this led-horse with all that truck from Don Carlos's ranch loaded onto it is bad enough, and you just shutting your jaws up like a clam don't make things any better."

"I've been too busy thinking to do much talking," Longarm answered. "And if you're wondering about what's going to happen to you, I ain't got the least idea yet. We'll both find out at the same time when we get there, which won't be too much of a long time now."

He motioned toward the buildings that were coming into sight on the long downslope that stretched beyond the low ridge they'd just topped after a long hour of hard uphill riding. Their horses were breathing hard and slowing down, especially the borrowed led-horse loaned them by Adelita; it was carrying the heavy coin molds and brass rounds that Longarm had removed from the shed for evidence before blowing it up.

Longarm went on. "Now since we started out, this is maybe ten times you've poked that question at me. We hadn't got a mile away from Don Carlos O'Riley's ranch before you asked me that the first time."

"Well, a man's got a right to know something about what's going to happen to him," Timmons insisted.

"It's downright hard to tell you something that I don't know myself," Longarm pointed out. "Because I can't see no way of telling you about what I ain't figured out yet for myself. But you'll find out soon as I get everything together. And that won't be till I've talked around a little bit."

"Talked to who?" Timmons asked.

"I don't figure that's any affair of yours," Longarm told him. "But I got this much to say, even if it ain't going to make you feel much better."

"Meaning what?" Timmons asked.

"Meaning that I don't aim to turn you over to nobody that's likely to let go of you any time soon," Longarm said.

"Sounds to me like you're talking about jail now," Timmons protested.

"Don't jump off no bridges till you get to 'em." Longarm's voice was firm, but it held neither threat nor anger. "Now, suppose you just set your mind at rest, because things got a way of settling down right side up."

This time Timmons made no comment and asked no more questions. During their long conversation they'd reached the first straggle of houses that marked Monterrey's beginning. They rode on in silence until they reached the center of town. The day was well along now. The bottom rim of the reddened sun was just touching the rooflines of the buildings.

On the streets, the number of pedestrians was moderate, although a number of the stores and small narrow office buildings were either deserted or had already closed for the day. Longarm kept scanning their fronts as they rode slowly down the street until Timmons turned to him, a frown on his face.

"You looking for something special, Longarm? Or are you just admiring the scenery?" he asked. "I know you ain't just trying to find a restaurant because we already passed two or three of 'em. Damn it, every time I see a general store or a restaurant my belly starts yelling at me that it feels like my throat's been cut."

"You can't be much hungrier'n I am," Longarm replied. "But if it'll satisfy your curiosity, I'm looking for the American consul's office, if they got one here."

"Then why the hell didn't you ask me where it is?"

"Because I didn't figure you'd know much more about where it is than I do."

"Maybe I don't know about a lot of things in Monterrey," Timmons said. "But when I was on the run it just so happens that I came down here. That was a little while before I hired out to Don Carlos O'Riley. I didn't know how safe it was for me to go looking to the American consul's office for help, but I was sure tempted a time or two. Anyhow, that's how come I know where the place is."

"Then suppose you tell me which way to go," Longarm suggested. "It'll likely save us some time."

"It's two streets over from this one we're on, and we've already passed it, so we'll have to backtrack."

Longarm nodded without saying anything that might prolong the exchange between him and his prisoner. They reached the next intersecting street and he reined into it. When they'd passed one intersection and were approaching the second he saw the United States flag on a staff that angled out from a second-floor window a short distance away.

"It strikes me that you know your way around this place pretty good," Longarm remarked. "Did you stay very long a time when you landed here before?"

"I was here long enough to find my way around without too much trouble," Timmons answered. "And that was time enough for me to get acquainted with Don Carlos."

"You told me you just run into him, but you never did say how or when," Longarm noted. "Did you go looking for a job, or was he looking for a man that could work gold?"

"Now I guess I never did tell you all about that," Timmons said. "It was at a bullfight, and I never had been to one before. I was setting next to him and I made a few remarks, not to him, just talking to myself, and he begun correcting me when I said something wrong. Then we got to talking, and it all wound up with him hiring me."

"So that's how you got tied up in his fake-gold-piece deal," Longarm said. "I been sorta wondering how that all come about."

They'd now reached the narrow two-story building where the flag was displayed. Its facade was anything but imposing: a door in the center flanked by two high-set windows, both of them bearing signs, one in English, one in Spanish, identifying it as the United States consulate.

"It ain't that I don't trust you to stay outside here and keep an eye on our horses and gear while I go inside," Longarm told him as they reined to a halt in front of the building. "But I don't aim to let my saddlebags outa my sight for a minute, not with all them things in 'em that I need for evidence. Suppose you carry 'em and come along with me. Then if you got anything you feel like saying to that consul, you'll be handy."

While Longarm was talking he and Timmons had dismounted and secured their horses to the hitch post. Longarm lifted off his saddlebags and handed them to Timmons. Side by side they walked to the door of the consulate. Longarm was just reaching for the knob when the door swung open and a man stepped out. A frown swept his face when he saw Longarm and Timmons.

"I'm afraid you gentlemen have gotten here too late if you're here on consular business," he said. "The consul himself has already left, and so have all the clerks."

"Well, you ain't left yet," Longarm said. "You work here, don't you?"

"Of course. I'm Edward Randall, the assistant consul."

"And I'm a deputy United States marshal," Longarm said. He fished out his badge and held it for Randall to examine as he went on. "Name's Long, Custis Long, outa the Denver office. I'd imagine we got pretty much the same boss back in Washington, and seeing as how

138

that's the way things are, it looks like you oughta take a minute or so to oblige me."

Randall's head had jerked up when he heard the word "Washington." He hesitated for only a moment before replying, "I'm sure you wouldn't describe your case as important unless that's really the situation, Marshal Long. Suppose you come inside with me and explain what's involved."

"If I go with you, this man here's got to come in too," Longarm said. "Because he's part of the case I was sent here on, besides being a prisoner that I got to keep my eye on."

"Then by all means bring him with you," Randall said. "We can discuss this case of yours, and when I find out exactly what's involved, I'll see what I can do to help you."

Longarm nudged Timmons to go through the door ahead of him, and the consular assistant stepped aside to let them pass. He closed the door and locked it, then gestured toward a desk behind the long counter that spanned the length of the narrow room.

"We can use one of the clerks' desks," he said. "My office is upstairs, and I can't see any reason now for going to it."

"If it's all the same to you, I'd as lief stand up," Longarm told him. He reached for the saddlebags Timmons was carrying and dropped them with a heavy thunk beside the desk where Timmons had settled.

"From the weight of those saddlebags, I'd say you've been carrying a pretty heavy load," Randall remarked as Longarm sat down. "If you've ridden very far today I can understand why you might be anxious to wind up whatever sort of business has brought you here."

"Oh, they're heavy, all right," Longarm agreed. "They oughta be. If you're curious about 'em, they're loaded with a lot of evidence that I've picked up while I was closing this case that I was sent on down here."

"Now if you're here on a criminal case, I don't intend to ask too many questions," Randall said. "So suppose you tell me what's brought you to our office."

"Mainly, what's in these saddlebags," Longarm began. "And like I said a minute ago, this fellow that's with me, he's a prisoner I'm taking back across the border. The thing is, I still got a mite of digging to do here in Monterrey, and for all I know I might wind up having to travel some more. What I need is a place I can leave him and the evidence in the bags where I'm certain-sure they'll be safe."

Randall did not reply for a moment. Then he said, "I suppose you've thought about asking the *rurales* to keep him in custody until you're ready to go back?"

"Now, that's about the last thing I'd be fool enough to do," Longarm replied. "Because me and the *rurales* ain't on what you'd call speaking terms."

"You've had trouble with them then?" Randall asked.

"I reckon you'd call it that," Longarm replied. "I had to gun down a couple of them right after I got here. They nabbed me and took me to their private lockup. Then they began asking a lot of questions about my case. When I didn't tell 'em, they squeezed my hand pretty good in a tricky kind of iron glove, and I had to shoot 'em to get free. Now, I know they got a shit list, and I figure my name's right up at the top of it."

An expression of incredulity had formed on Randall's face while Longarm talked. "You're saying that you killed two *rurales* here in Monterrey and walked away scot-free?"

"That's the size of it," Longarm replied.

"I'd surely have heard about something like that," Randall said. "We have some private sources of information here at the consulate, and I don't see how we could've missed learning about an American shooting two of Mexico's best—"

Longarm broke in. "Just a minute, Mr Randall. Like you started to say, the *rurales* are about as good law officers as you'll find, but when you got on a blindfold and go to put meat in a stew, there's bound to be some rotten spots. Anyways, the *rurales* have got their own way of doing things. Now begging your pardon in advance, let's get back to what I come here for. There's some things I got to do here yet, and I need to get on with 'em. I'd appreciate it if we can get this business finished, because I need to get back to this case I'm working."

"Exactly what do you expect us to do?" Randall asked.

"Why it won't be such a much," Longarm answered. "All I need right this minute is for you to take custody of my prisoner."

"Now hold on, Longarm!" Timmons objected. "You didn't say a word to me about that! How do I know—"

"No, you hold on!" Longarm snapped. "I been treating you the best I know how to, because I want you to be a witness in whatever case my chief and the government lawyers make against Don Carlos O'Riley. You knew that right from the start."

Timmons did not reply for a moment. Then he nodded and said, "I guess you're right. I stepped out of line."

Turning back to Randall, Longarm went on. "Mainly what I want you to do is to keep this fellow safe and sound until I'm ready to take him back across the border with me."

"Well, even though we don't have prison cells or anything like them, I'm sure we can find a way to do that," Randall said slowly. "Even though it's not one of our customary procedures."

Longarm nodded. "And I got some evidence for you to hold on to till I can start back."

"What sort of evidence?"

"Molds that counterfeiters have been using to make fake United States double eagles with, and a bunch of fake coins and some other little truck that goes with my case. I reckon you got a safe that'll be big enough to hold 'em?"

When the diplomat answered, his voice showed his relief. "Of course. If that's all you need, we won't have any trouble accommodating you. I'm sure we can keep them securely until you need them. Now, is there anything else?"

"Well, there's a couple of horses outside, but I can put them in the stable at the Hotel del Norte. That's where I'll be stopping. But there ain't nothing else that comes to mind right now," Longarm replied. "Except I want you keep this fellow safe till I come back to get him."

"Don't worry," Randall said quickly. "Now that I know how much is involved with your case I'll be very careful. You'll find him ready when you want him again."

Reining his horse away from the embassy and leading Timmons's mount, Longarm rode to the Hotel del Norte. Monterrey's streets were almost deserted now, and his ride was mercifully short. He made short work of checking in at the hotel and seeking the bathroom across the corridor from his own room. Refreshed after getting rid of the thick layer of trail dust accumulated during the ride to and from O'Riley's ranch and the mine, he dressed quickly and strapped on his gunbelt. Then he made his way to Benito's small *cantina*. To his pleased surprise, he saw Benito was alone. There were no customers at the bar nor any of the tables.

"Brazolargo!" Benito greeted him. "Ees good for to see you again. Wait *un momento,* I weel get your bottle, then we weel talk." Stepping to the shelf where the almost empty bottle of Tom Moore rested, he filled a shot glass and placed it before Longarm. Then he said, "You do well on your case, I am to hope? Or should not I ask of your beesiness matters?"

"Well now, you ain't going to hear me complaining," Longarm replied. He took a swallow of the liquor and replaced the glass on the counter, then raised his arm in a gesture to take in the empty room. "But was I in your shoes, I just might. Where's all of your customers?"

Shrugging, Benito replied. "They are *laborares, trabajadores.* Thees ees time work ees not easy to find. They have no *dinero* to speend weeth me. But eet weel change, thees I have learned."

"As long as you ain't hurting, Nito, I guess you're glad to get a bit of rest," Longarm said. "There's times when I like a little bit of time away from my job too."

"Your case ees closed theen?"

"Not quite," Longarm answered. "I still got a few loose ends to pick up."

"For a while, theen, you weel be here?"

"Oh, sure. I got one more puzzle to work out, then maybe I can close it up."

"Thees puzzle you have, can you tell me of it?"

"Sure. Besides having a little talk with you and getting a drink of decent whiskey, that's one reason I come in tonight."

Gesturing toward the deserted bar and unoccupied tables, Benito said, "Weeth no *clientes,* we have the time to talk."

"Well, mostly I need to find out about the bad side of Monterrey," Longarm went on. "I got a hunch that Don Carlos O'Riley ain't going show his face at that bank of his, and I can't stay here forever."

"You weesh to arrest heem theen?" Benito asked.

"I sure do. But I can't stay here forever, trying to run him to earth. Now, I'll be going to that fancy new bank of his tomorrow, but I ain't really looking to find him there."

"You theenk he ees hide?"

Longarm nodded. "I got a hunch that Don Carlos has got a lot more up his sleeve than he's ever showed."

"Weeth what you theenk, I am agree," Benito said.

"I got all the evidence I need to arrest him and haul him back across the border with me. Trouble is, I don't know enough about this town to figure where he might be hiding out."

Benito was silent for a thoughtful moment, then he said, "*Los túneles.* Thees ees where you weel find heem."

"*Túneles?*" Longarm repeated. "You're talking about tunnels? Where in tunket would I go looking for 'em?"

"Wheen first eet e-start, Monterrey ees beeg mining town," Benito said. "Ees all below eet *túneles* een ground. They are many, go all thees way, that way. *Los ladrones* are hide een theem. Even *los rurales* do not go een theem alone."

For a moment Longarm was silent. Then he said, "I reckon you know a little bit about 'em, the way you talk. You reckon you could tell me how to find my way around 'em?"

Benito shook his head. "To tell you ees not possible, Brazolargo." After only a moment's hesitation he went on. "But I weel go weeth you eef you are weesh to go to *los túneles* and look for your prisoner."

Chapter 13

A thoughtful frown formed on Longarm's face as he stood for a moment staring silently at Benito. At last he asked, "You really mean what you just said, Nito?"

Benito shrugged as he answered. "*Seguro*. Eef I am not to mean eet, I do not say eet."

"I oughta know you well enough by now not to ask a fool question like that," Longarm said with a smile. Then his face grew sober. "And I sure thank you for what you've offered to do. But before you say any more, I got to tell you that I can't ask you to go along."

"You have not to ask," Benito reminded him quickly. "I am the one who offers."

"It's my job we're talking about, not yours."

"Please do not to make the foolish talk, Brazolargo. Eef I do not go weeth you, maybe so you get lost een *los túneles*, and eef you are alone, maybe so too the *ladrones* are to keel you."

"Well, I might have something to say about that, but I can tell when you got your head made up," Longarm told him. "So I ain't going to argue. Come along and welcome, Nito. I'll be right proud to have a good man like you with me. Just go ahead and figure out when the best time is to drop down into them tunnels and we'll start out."

"Ees best we go wheen ees just start daytime," Benito suggested. "Een night, *los ladrones,* they are come up to streets because night ees time when they are e-steal easiest. Theen when ees close to rising the sun they go back to *los túneles.* The daytime ees wheen they e-sleep."

"That being the case, I'd say tomorrow morning'd be the time to take our look-see," Longarm said thoughtfully. "And I could stand a good sleep in a real bed tonight." He drained the last few drops remaining in his glass and stood up. "Suppose I come and meet you here a little while before sun up. Then we'll go see what we can turn up on the bottom side of Monterrey."

Dawn was just beginning to brighten the eastern sky when Longarm left the hotel. He stopped outside the door to cradle his rifle in his elbow as he lighted a cigar. Its wispy smoke trail wavered behind him in the clear morning air as he walked unhurriedly to the little saloon. Light streaming from its windows told him that Benito was waiting. Pushing through the door, he saw Benito sitting at one of the rear tables, an empty plate in front of him.

"*Hola,* Longarm," Benito said. He gestured toward the table. "You are eat *el desayuno,* no?"

"Not so's you'd notice, Nito. I found out that hotel don't begin putting out grub this early," Longarm replied.

147

"But I figured you might have a bite or two that I could eat for breakfast. Now, I ain't one bit choosy about what it is, just anything you got on hand that'll stop my belly from griping."

Benito nodded and gestured toward the chair opposite him as he said, "I am theenk of thees. A small breakfast I have kept waiting for you."

"I don't mind telling you, it'll sure be welcome. There ain't nothing worse'n a man heading out on an empty stomach when he's starting the kinda job we got coming up."

"From the way you e-speak, I theenk maybe so you have been een old mines before," Benito said as he placed a napkin-covered plate on the table in front of Longarm.

"Well, I been in one or two old closed-down mines on a few cases I've worked," Longarm said. "But not any of 'em lately, and a course I never was in this one we'll be going to."

By this time Benito had removed the napkin; the plate held three fat *enchiladas* topped by shreds of cheese. "Eat well," he told Longarm. "We maybe weel be in *los túneles* for all the day, so I have make leetle *comida* we are to take weeth us. But thees ees day I buy food for three, four days ahead, so in *la despensa* I have but leetle."

"That won't bother me none. Nito. Anyways, I don't figure it oughta take us too long to do our job, because in the mines that I was in I never did see one that's had too much ground to cover. But from what I've found out about caves and old mine-diggings and such, there don't seem to be no two alike."

"About others, I do not know," Benito said as Longarm started eating. "But of one theeng I am e-sure, we weel have to e-stay close together. Only those who know well

148

the *túneles* can move weethout care een them."

By taking oversized bites, Longarm finished eating quickly. He pushed away his empty plate and eased his chair back from the table before lighting a fresh cigar. When it was drawing to his satisfaction he looked questioningly at Benito.

"I guess we're ready as we ever will be," Longarm said, reaching for his rifle. "So if you feel like pushing off, I'll be right alongside of you."

"Eet ees good enough time as eeny," Benito agreed. "But do not breeng the long gun, Brazolargo."

"You don't figure we'll need it if we run into trouble?"

"Ees not thees," Benito replied, shaking his head. "*El fusil* ees not good een *los túneles*. Ees shoot so loud as to make top to fall down on us. I have good knife. Eet weel be all we need to keep *los brutos* from harm us."

"I hadn't given that a thought," Longarm told him. "But I can see you're right. I guess my Winchester'll be safe enough if I leave it here in your place?"

"*Seguro,*" Benito assured him. "I weel put it under bar. Eet weel be safe there." He tucked the rifle away and gestured toward the door. "*Pasaremos.* Thees place where we are going into *los túneles* ees not from here very far."

At this early hour Monterrey's streets were still almost deserted when Longarm and Benito started from the restaurant. The sun had not yet come up, but the brightening light of the eastern sky showed that it would appear soon. They walked along Zaragoza Street, and neared the scattering of buildings that dotted the center around the governmental palace. As they reached it, Benito nodded toward the imposing building that rose above the smaller structures.

149

"We are go to back of el Palacio Municipal," he said. "Ees beeg joke on *gobierno*. The place where we go een *los túneles* ees so close by where is office of the *policía*. We go yet only leetle way to reach eet."

They moved on beyond the government building, and Benito pointed to a faint trail that ran from the street to the rear of the government building. Benito turned off the roadway, gesturing for Longarm to follow. Longarm fell in behind him on the almost invisible trail. They wound along it in silence until it came to an abrupt end at a steep drop-off only a scant quarter mile past the municipal building.

Stepping up to the edge of the ledge, Benito scanned the rolling meadowland below for a moment. Then before Longarm could reach his companion, Benito had stepped off the edge of the bluff and with his legs straddled wide took short quick steps as he descended its steep downgrade. When Longarm followed it seemed to him as though a lariat was pulling at him during their descent, but by twisting and turning to keep his balance he was still standing upright as he skidded to a stop beside Benito.

Longarm looked along the face of the tall ledge they'd just descended, but could see nothing that resembled an opening. He turned to Benito, but before he could ask the question he'd intended to, Benito motioned to their left along the face of the rise.

"Thees way," he said. "Ees very close now, the way een to *los túneles*."

Even before he'd finished speaking, Benito was turning to lead the way along the foot of the bluff. Longarm followed him in silence, noting carefully the landmarks that he might need to use in finding the way back. Their walk was surprisingly short. It ended at a point where a boulder the size of a small house protruded from the face of the bluff. Beyond the boulder the face of the abrupt rise was broken by a jagged black gap.

At first glance the opening seemed to be a mere crack, too small to allow a man to squeeze into it. Then Longarm took another step or two past the raw rock face and saw the gaping slit that opened between the boulder and the wall. Benito extended his arm to keep Longarm from going closer.

"We wait *un momento*," he said. "Eef ees coming from een-side anybody, we hear theem first." After they'd listened for a moment and no noise broke the silence he said, "Ees safe. I weel go een, you come after me."

"Now, hold on!" Longarm protested. "It's my case we're here on, Nito, so I oughta take whatever chances pop up."

"I know better what ees to leesten for," Benito reminded him. "Ees small, the chance from danger."

Without waiting for Longarm to reply, and without giving him a chance to enter first, Benito stepped past him and disappeared in the blackness beyond the boulder. Longarm hurried to follow. The change from the beginning day's brightness to the blank darkness that lay beyond caused him to blink. Then as he stopped beside Benito, his eyes began to adjust to the gloom and he found that he could see a few yards ahead.

To Longarm's surprise the tunnel's floor in the area they'd now reached was broken at intervals by crudely hewn lengths of wood. Then he recalled Benito's remark about the tunnels having at one time been a mine, or series of mines. The memory of one of the mines he'd visited where small ore carts ran on narrow tracks flashed through his mind as Benito stopped suddenly. Longarm halted beside him.

Benito gestured toward the base of the tunnel just ahead of them as he said in a low whisper, "Walk e-softly and be very quiet as we are go by theem."

Longarm's eyes were accustomed to the darkness by now, and when he looked in the direction his companion had indicated he saw a half-dozen large bundles lying on the floor against the base of the wall. Then he realized that the shapeless huddles were people, but in the gloom he could not tell whether they were men or women.

"Eef they are to wake, they are to see very queek we are not of their kind," Benito whispered. "But there are those who are *Bandidos, ladrones*. Maybe so they are to fight us so they can e-steal what we have."

"Well, I ain't looking to fight with nobody but Don Carlos O'Riley, if he's hiding out down here," Longarm replied. He followed Benito's example, and spoke in a barely audible tone. "But I don't figure he's the kind of man that'd bunk down on a dirt floor."

"Thees ees true thing," Benito agreed. "But here ees mostly *desechos,* trash. We are not yet get to place where *bandidos* e-stay. Eet ees more deeper een *los túneles*."

Moving slowly and carefully, Benito turned and resumed his slow advance, Longarm following a step behind him. As they progressed, they passed a number of solitary sleepers as well as other small groups similar to the first, from three or four people to perhaps as many as a dozen. In many of the groups they saw one or two who were sitting erect, but they were staring into the gloom, ignoring Longarm and Benito as though they did not exist.

After covering what seemed to Longarm to be a long stretch, he and Benito drew close to one of the solitary sleepers. Both Longarm and Benito glanced at him as they passed, but before they'd taken more than two steps

Longarm heard the faint sound of booted feet scraping in the earth.

Longarm's reaction was instantaneous. He drew his Colt as he whirled around. He saw that the man who'd appeared to be asleep was on his feet now, lunging forward with a glinting steel knife in his hand. Even before Benito reacted to the threat, Longarm's Colt barked. The assailant jerked erect as the slug slammed into his chest. His extended knife hand froze, the glistening blade's needle-sharp point still a full arm's length away from Longarm.

Then the dying outlaw's knife hand sagged and the deadly blade slid to the ground, its point digging into the tunnel's floor to hold it erect. The would-be killer took a single tottering backward step before crumpling to his knees and lurching forward to fall upon his own knife. Another convulsive shudder shook him as he landed and lay motionless.

For a moment neither Benito nor Longarm spoke. Then Benito said, "You have lost none of your skill with the gun, Brazolargo. But we must look more closely at those we see as we go further. There are many more like him in the *túneles*."

"Oh, I ain't got no doubts at all about that, Nito," Longarm said. He was thumbing in a fresh shell from his gunbelt as he spoke. While he ejected the used shell case from the Colt's cylinder and reloaded he went on. "Just like I didn't have none about what you told me about this place. But what are we going to do about that dead man laying there?"

"We do nothing. All people down here are scavengers. They will take hees clothes, theen they weel bury heem."

"Well, it seems sorta cold-hearted to me," Longarm said. "But if it's the custom of the country, I ain't going

153

to be the one that tries to change it. Let's just go on about our business."

Silently they resumed their steady progress along the tunnel. They'd walked for only a few minutes when suddenly the dirt floor ended and a stretch of brick paving on the tunnel's floor stretched ahead of them, where the darkness was diluted by a glimmer of subdued light from the ceiling. Though the glow was feeble, Longarm's eyes were so accustomed to the gloom through which he and Benito had passed that when they reached the dimly lighted section, its glimmer of brightness gave them the illusion that they were entering a zone of daylight.

"Do not have the surprise," Benito said. "Eet is light from *desaguardero,* what you call drain from street. Ees old. There are few left from time wheen all Monterrey streets have mud so deep we are not walk, we sweem. Now streets have breeks, but old drains are not e-stop up."

"How come you know so much about these tunnels and rooms down here, Nito?" Longarm asked.

"Because I e-see much of eet wheen ees being built, wheen I am *niño,*" Benito replied.

"And I reckon none of us forgets what we seen when we was yunkers. I know I . . ." Longarm stopped without finishing his remark as they rounded a slanting bend in the tunnel and saw a door that closed the passage a few steps ahead of them. The door looked very solid. It was made from narrow grooved vertical boards and had an imposingly large brass knob set in a thick escutcheon plate. Longarm went on. "If I ain't wrong, we've got to the place we been heading for."

Benito nodded as they stopped in front of the door. Gesturing to Longarm to remain silent, he stepped up and grasped the brass doorknob. He tried to turn the knob, but it did not move. Turning back to face Longarm, Benito shook his head.

"*Es trabado,*" he told Longarm. "Lock tight like anytheeng. And ees so theek we are not have way to—"

Benito broke off as a key grated in the lock and the door swung open. Don Carlos O'Riley stood in the doorway. He did not speak, but the fancy silver-plated revolver in his hand made words unnecessary. O'Riley was fanning the gun in slow short arcs to threaten both Longarm and Benito.

Longarm recognized O'Riley's moves. They were the same ones that he used himself when covering two men with his Colt or Winchester. He stood motionless, his ice-blue eyes flicking from Don Carlos's face to the glistening silvery revolver. Beside Longarm, Benito had also frozen. Except for O'Riley's threatening motion with his revolver neither of the three men moved.

"So," O'Riley said, "We meet once more. I cannot say how pleased I am."

"And I'm right glad to see you, Don Carlos," Longarm told the *hacendado*. "Now I've found you, I won't have to meander around looking for you no more."

"You speak brave words, even if you must know you will not escape me again," O'Riley said. His voice bore the chill of an icy winter wind sweeping down from a snowcapped mountain as he continued. "Though how you managed to escape from my trusted helper at my mine and find me here, I do not know."

"Oh, getting free wasn't such a much of a job," Longarm told him. In spite of the threatening revolver in Don Carlos's hand, Longarm's voice was level, almost casual. "And I already knew you had business here in Monterrey, likely at your bank, so I just tagged along after you."

155

O'Riley's voice dripped sarcasm as he asked, "I am sure that my loving wife told you of my decision to return to Monterrey?" When Longarm did not answer, but kept his eyes fixed on the gun in Don Carlos's hand, the *hacendado* continued. "Or was it one of my servants that I depended on to be faithful to me who told you?"

"Nobody needed to tell me anything," Longarm replied. "You told me yourself at the mine."

"And I am sure you lie!" O'Riley snapped. "Just as I am sure that this *peon* with you has led you here."

"Maybe I am *peon*!" Benito retorted. "But I do not lie or e-steal as you do, Don Carlos! *Sí,* I am help my friend Brazolargo to find you, but he has told me of your cruelty and your thieving. Now, what do you say to that?"

For a moment Longarm thought that Don Carlos was going to trigger his revolver, but though the hacendado's face twisted in anger, he did not shoot. The ugly scowl faded and a saturnine smile formed to replace it.

"We waste time talking," he said. "And at this moment I have no time for your *tontería*. You will both come into this room and sit in the chairs I choose for you."

Longarm and Benito exchanged covert glances, and Longarm nodded almost imperceptibly. Then they moved forward while Don Carlos slowly fanned the muzzle of his revolver from side to side in order to cover first one of them, then the other. He stepped into the corridor and gestured for Longarm and Benito to enter the room.

As they moved to obey Don Carlos's orders Longarm got his first really good look at the chamber. It was large and the effects of age were apparent at a glance, but its size alone told Longarm that at one time it must have been used for some purpose of importance.

Though the chamber's ceiling was low and bore water stains that marked old leaks, both it and the walls were decorated with faded murals picturing the activities of both workers and scholars. The *peones* wore only loincloths and widebrimmed hats as they did such jobs as planting seeds and building small houses. The scholars in their dark-hued robes were reading from enormous books and writing with quill pens on sheets of parchment.

Longarm gave these details only cursory attention. He took no more than a quick glance at the pictures before returning his inspection to the massive table that occupied the room's center. The tabletop was almost entirely covered with gold coins and small scattered leather bags. Some of the coins had been placed in neatly lined-up stacks, but many more of them were heaped in a pile in the center. Don Carlos noticed Longarm's stare, and when he spoke again there was menace in the tone of his voice.

"I am sure you must see why I am angry that you have discovered one of my secrets," he said. "And I do not take you for a fool. You must understand that because of what you have found, both you and your companion must die."

Chapter 14

Longarm did not reply at once to Don Carlos O'Riley's threat. He kept his eyes fixed on the menacing revolver for a moment before lifting his head to exchange stares with their captor. Nodding in unhurried deliberation, he said, "Well now, Don Carlos, you ain't said nothing that surprises me. It's just about what I'd figure a man like you to come up with."

"You think I do not have the courage to shoot you?"

Ignoring the question, Longarm went on. "Why, it don't take much backbone to pull a trigger. Especially when you're talking to a man that's looking right down the muzzle of your pistol and he ain't got a gun in his hand."

"Do you dare to suggest that I am a coward?" Don Carlos asked. As he waited for a reply he shifted the muzzle of his revolver to threaten Longarm more directly than Benito. When he saw that Longarm did not intend to respond to his question, O'Riley continued. "By this time you must have learned enough about me to know that I do not allow anyone—not you or any other man on earth—to interfere with my plans."

"You can take what I said any way you feel like, Don Carlos," Longarm said calmly. While he was speaking Longarm was also searching his mind for a reply that might irritate his adversary enough to distract him and slow down his reactions. "But all I got to say is that you're what folks down here call *desechos*."

"You insult me!" the rancher exclaimed when he heard Longarm describe him as trash. His voice was strained almost to the point of choking, and instead of swiveling the muzzle of his revolver to cover both Longarm and Benito, he held it fixed on Longarm.

For a fleeting instant Longarm was tempted to respond to the implied challenge in Don Carlos's move by drawing his Colt and firing as he dropped to the ground. Then common sense dominated as Longarm's finely honed and almost instinctive lawman's reaction warned him that the time had not yet come for a final showdown. As long as Carlos was balanced on a knife-blade edge, even the slightest movement to draw would be recklessly foolish. A premature move now might well result in spoiling a better opportunity to escape later.

At that instant Benito's voice broke the tense silence. "No, Brazolargo!" he exclaimed. "Don Carlos is *hidalgo*! He would not do a thing so cowardly as to shoot us when our hands are empty of weapons to threaten him!"

During the brief second or two of tension that followed Benito's outburst, O'Riley stood motionless. Then he shrugged, and the tone of his voice altered subtly as he replied. "Perhaps you and the boy are both right in the names you call me. But I promise you now that you will not trick me by using insults. No matter what you say, it changes little except the time and place where you will die."

"We ain't looking for you to do us no favors," Longarm replied. "It's just that I'd a heap rather arrest you and haul you back to stand trial than shoot you."

"So you are a lawman after all!" Carlos snapped. "But you will do neither! Not unless you choose to try! If you do, I warn you again that you will die at once!"

Longarm could see that any opportunity to draw O'Riley into a moment of inattention had passed.

"Well now," he said. "It looks to me like we got a sorta standoff here. There's two of us and one of you, Don Carlos, but you're holding the gun, and that makes you the boss. Seeing as how I ain't ready to cash in my chips just yet, I'd say we ain't fixed to pick and choose. Maybe you'd like to tell us what you got in mind?"

Don Carlos did not reply for a moment. Then he gestured to the gold coins heaped on the table and said, "There is a small job to be done here, as you can see. It is not one that I care to do myself, and the man I have trusted to do it has suffered an accident. You and your companion will take his place."

"I ain't quite sure about what kind of a job you got in mind," Longarm said. "But seeing as how you got that gun in your hand, it sorta looks like there ain't much we can do but what you tell us to."

A gloating smile formed on O'Riley's face as he said, "I am glad to find that you understand your unfortunate position. As for the job, it is one which even a stupid *gringo* can do. Into each of these sacks you will count fifty gold pieces. That is the first part of your task. When the gold is counted, you will become my burros and carry it to the place where it must be delivered. That is the second part."

"Then I take what you just said to mean you're ready to send some more of them counterfeit double eagles into the United States?" Longarm asked.

"Of course," Don Carlos replied. "And it will give me much pleasure to see you forced to break the laws of your own country. It will be your dying memory, for when you have finished your work, I will have no more use for you."

"Brazolargo!" Benito exclaimed. "He weell keell us wheen we are feenish!"

"Talk's cheap," Longarm told his companion. "Anyways, we ain't got much choice right now but to do what he told us to."

"I am glad you have not forced me to kill you before now," Don Carlos said. "But to make sure that you perform your task properly, I will be watching you most closely. And I do not plan to holster my pistol. If you have in your mind to trick me, I will shoot you. Now go to the table there and do what I have told you!"

Longarm nodded to Benito. They moved to opposite sides of the table and sat down. Longarm picked up one of the leather bags and began counting the counterfeit coins into it. He moved slowly, handling only one coin at a time. Benito glanced at Longarm's slow moves and followed his example.

Without taking his eyes off Longarm and Benito and still covering them with his revolver, Don Carlos O'Riley snaked a chair up to one end of the table with his foot and settled into it. He kept his pistol in his hand, resting it on the top of the table. He watched Longarm and Benito for a few moments, then rapped the tabletop with the revolver's butt.

"Work more swiftly!" he commanded. "You do not fool me by trying to delay!"

Playing for time now, Longarm replied, "You got to remember, we ain't used to doing this kind of job. And you'd likely get mad as a wet hen, like you did a minute ago, if we didn't put just the right number of these fake double eagles into every one of these bags. If we didn't, I'd imagine that whoever the crooks are that lug 'em across the Rio Grande'd would likely get mad at you when they found out."

"Do as I tell you!" Don Carlos snapped. "Move faster!"

Both Longarm and Benito speeded up a bit. Don Carlos did not move, but kept shifting his eyes from one to the other to make sure his orders were being obeyed. Longarm filled one of the leather bags and pushed it across the table until it was in front of Don Carlos. He picked up another bag and began to fill it, but worked no more swiftly than he had before.

Don Carlos rapped the top of the table with his pistol butt. Then he said, "You do not obey me! You must work with better speed! Soon the men who will carry the bags across the Rio Grande will be here to get them!"

"We're doing the best we can," Longarm told him. "Like I just told you, this ain't the kind of work we do regular."

"Then learn to do it faster!" Don Carlos barked, his voice betraying his impatience.

"Whatever you say," Longarm replied.

He placed two more coins into the bag he'd been filling, and leaned forward to push it toward the few filled bags in front of the rancher. He was pushing with his left hand while his right was hidden below the edge of the table, slipping his stubby derringer from its hidden sheath.

When the derringer's butt was safely nestled in his right hand, Longarm gripped a corner of the bag with the fingers of his left and snapped it upward. A shower of the counterfeit gold pieces gushed from the bag's mouth, tinkling on the tabletop, rolling in a scattered golden flood toward Don Carlos.

"Que groseria!" the *hidalgo* exclaimed as he reached across the table with both hands, leaning forward as he tried to gather in the counterfeit gold pieces that were rolling toward him in a glittering golden stream.

Longarm raised the derringer to cover O'Riley as he said, "Just freeze right where you are, Don Carlos. I'd hate to have to use this gun on you, but if you—"

Longarm had no chance to finish his warning and no choice but to trigger the derringer. Its heavy slug smashed into Don Carlos's head. The impact of the big leaden slug pushed him backward and Don Carlos slumped to the floor, where he lay motionless, dead before his fall was completed.

For a moment after the reverberations of the shot echoed through the underground chamber, neither Longarm nor Benito spoke. They stood looking at Don Carlos's sprawled-out form on the floor of the underground chamber.

"If I am to know you are carry that gun, I am not to worry so much about us," Benito said at last. He gestured toward Don Carlos's body. "You are sure thees little *pistola* have keel heem?"

"Just as dead as a big one would," Longarm assured him. "But we ain't got time to talk about guns, Nito. There's a lot of clearing away to do after we get up to where it's daylight. And I don't mind telling you, I'll be real glad to knot up the last one because I got a real hankering to be looking back at Monterrey from the back coach of the first train I can take to get me back to Denver."

Watch for

LONGARM AND THE GUNSLICKS

160th in the bold
LONGARM series from Jove

Coming in April!

BOOK ONE
(1864–1867)

It is my unhappy lot to write the closing entry in this journal.

Clay Halser is dead, killed this morning in my presence.

I have known him since we met during the latter days of The War Between The States. I have run across him, on occasion, through ensuing years and am, in fact, partially responsible (albeit involuntarily) for a portion of the legend which has magnified around him.

It is for these reasons (and another more important) that I make this final entry.

I am in Silver Gulch acquiring research matter toward the preparation of a volume on the history of this territory (Colorado), which has recently become the thirty-eighth state of our Union.

I was having breakfast in the dining room of the *Silver Lode Hotel* when a man entered and sat down at a table across the room, his back to the wall. Initially, I failed to recognize him though there was, in his comportment, something familiar.

Several minutes later (to my startlement), I realized that it was none other than Clay Halser. True, I had not laid eyes on him for many years. Nonetheless, I was completely taken back by the change in his appearance.

I was not, at that point, aware of his age, but took it to be somewhere in the middle thirties. Contrary to this, he presented the aspect of a man at least a decade older.

His face was haggard, his complexion (in my memory, quite ruddy) pale to the point of being ashen. His eyes, formerly suffused with animation, now looked burned out, dead. What many horrific sights those eyes had beheld I could not—and cannot—begin to estimate. Whatever those sights, however, no evidence of them had been reflected in his eyes before; it was as though he'd been emotionally immune.

He was no longer so. Rather, one could easily imagine that his eyes were gazing, in that very moment, at those bloody sights, dredging from the depths within his mind to which he'd relegated them, all their awful measure.

From the standpoint of physique, his deterioration was equally marked. I had always known him as a man of vigorous health, a condition necessary to sustain him in the execution of his harrowing duties. He was not a tall man; I would gauge his height at five feet ten inches maximum, perhaps an inch or so less, since his upright carriage and customary dress of black suit, hat, and boots might have afforded him the look of standing taller than he did. He had always been extremely well-presented though, with a broad chest, narrow waist, and pantherlike grace of movement; all in all, a picture of vitality.

Now, as he ate his meal across from me, I felt as though, by some bizarre transfiguration, I was gazing at an old man.

He had lost considerable weight and his dark suit (it, too, seemed worn and past its time) hung loosely on his frame. To my further disquiet, I noted a threading of gray through his dark blonde hair and saw a tremor in his hands completely foreign to the young man I had known.

I came close to summary departure. To my shame, I nearly chose to leave rather than accost him. Despite the congenial relationship I had enjoyed with him throughout the past decade, I found myself so totally dismayed by the alteration in his looks that I lacked the will to rise and cross the room to him, preferring to consider hasty exit. (I discovered, later, that the reason he had failed to notice me was that his vision, always so acute before, was now inordinately weak.)

At last, however, girding up my will, I stood and moved across the dining room, attempting to fix a smile of pleased surprise on my lips and hoping he would not be too aware of my distress.

"Well, good morning, Clay," I said, as evenly as possible.

I came close to baring my deception at the outset for, as he looked up sharply at me, his expression one of taut alarm, a perceptible "tic" under his right eye, I was hard put not to draw back apprehensively.

Abruptly, then, he smiled (though it was more a ghost of the smile I remembered). "*Frank*," he said and jumped to his feet. No, that is not an accurate description of his movement. It may well have been his intent to jump up and welcome me with avid handshake. As it happened, his stand was labored, his hand grip lacking in strength. "How *are* you?" he inquired. "It is good to see you."

"I'm fine," I answered.

"Good." He nodded, gesturing toward the table. "Join me."

I hope my momentary hesitation passed his notice. "I'd be happy to," I told him.

"Good," he said again.

We each sat down, he with his back toward the wall again. As we did, I noted how his gaunt frame slumped into the chair, so different from the movement of his earlier days.

He asked me if I'd eaten breakfast.

"Yes." I pointed across the room. "I was finishing when you entered."

"I am glad you came over," he said.

There was a momentary silence. Uncomfortable, I tried to think of something to say.

He helped me out. (I wonder, now, if it was deliberate; if he had, already, taken note of my discomfort.) "Well, old fellow," he asked, "what brings you to this neck of the woods?"

I explained my presence in Silver Gulch and, as I did, being now so close to him, was able to distinguish, in detail, the astounding metamorphosis which time (and experience) had effected.

There seemed to be, indelibly impressed on his still handsome face, a look of unutterable sorrow. His former blitheness had completely vanished and it was oppressive to behold what had occurred to his expression, to see the palsied gestures of his hands as he spoke, perceive the constant shifting of his eyes as though he was anticipating that, at any second, some impending danger might be thrust upon him.

I tried to coerce myself not to observe these things, concentrating on the task of bringing him "up to date" on my activities since last we'd met; no match for his activities, God knows.

"What about you?" I finally asked; I had no more to say about myself. "What are you doing these days?"

"Oh, gambling," he said, his listless tone indicative of his regard for that pursuit.

"No marshaling anymore?" I asked.

He shook his head. "Strictly the circuit," he answered.

"Circuit?" I wasn't really curious but feared the onset of silence and spoke the first word that occurred to me.

"A league of boomtown havens for faro players," he replied. "South Texas up to South Dakota—Idaho to Arizona. There is money to be gotten everywhere. Not that I am good enough to make a raise. And not that it's important if I do, at any rate. I only gamble for something to do."

All the time he spoke, his eyes kept shifting, searching; was it *waiting*?

As silence threatened once again, I quickly spoke. "Well, you have traveled quite a long road since the War," I said. "A long, exciting road." I forced a smile. "*Adventurous*," I added.

His answering smile was as sadly bitter and exhausted as any I have ever witnessed. "Yes, the writers of the stories have made it all sound very colorful," he said. He leaned back with a heavy sigh, regarding me. "I even thought it so myself at one time. Now I recognize it all for what it was." There was a tightening around his eyes. "Frank, it was drab, and dirty, and there was a lot of blood."

I had no idea how to respond to that and, in spite of my resolve, let silence fall between us once more.

Silence broke in a way that made my flesh go cold. A young man's voice behind me, from some distance in the room. "So that is him," the voice said loudly. "Well, he does not look like much to me."

I'd begun to turn when Clay reached out and gripped my arm. "Don't bother looking," he instructed me. "It's best to ignore them. I have found the more attention paid, the more difficult they are to shake in the long run."

He smiled but there was little humor in it. "Don't be concerned," he said. "It happens all the time. They spout a while, then go away, and brag that Halser took their guff and never did a thing. It makes them feel important. I don't mind. I've grown accustomed to it."

At which point, the boy—I could now tell, from the timbre of his voice, that he had not attained his majority—spoke again.

"He looks like nothing at all to me to be so all-fired famous a fighter with his guns," he said.

I confess the hostile quaver of his voice unsettled me. Seeing my reaction, Clay smiled and was about to speak when the boy—perhaps seeing the smile and angered by it—added, in a tone resounding enough to be heard in the lobby, "In fact, I believe he looks like a woman-hearted coward, that is what he looks like to me!"

"Don't worry now," Clay reassured me. "He'll blow himself out of steam presently and crawl away." I felt some sense of relief to see a glimmer of the old sauce in his eyes. "Probably to visit, with uncommon haste, the nearest outhouse."

Still, the boy kept on with stubborn malice. "My name is Billy Howard," he announced. "And I am going to make . . ."

He went abruptly mute as Clay unbuttoned his dark frock coat to reveal a butt-reversed Colt at his left side.

174

It was little wonder. Even I, a friend of Clay's, felt a chill of premonition at the movement. What spasm of dread it must have caused in the boy's heart, I can scarcely imagine.

"Sometimes I have to go this far," Clay told me. "Usually I wait longer but, since you are with me . . ." He let the sentence go unfinished and lifted his cup again.

I wanted to believe the incident was closed but, as we spoke—me asking questions to distract my mind from its foreboding state—I seemed to feel the presence of the boy behind me like some constant wraith.

"How are all your friends?" I asked.

"Dead," Clay answered.

"*All* of them?"

He nodded. "Yes. Jim Clements. Ben Pickett. John Harris."

I saw a movement in his throat. "Henry Blackstone. All of them."

I had some difficulty breathing. I kept expecting to hear the boy's voice again. "What about your wife?" I asked.

"I have not heard from her in some time," he replied. "We are estranged."

"How old is your daughter now?"

"Three in January," he answered, his look of sadness deepening. I regretted having asked and quickly said, "What about your family in Indiana?"

"I went back to visit them last year," he said. "It was a waste."

I did not want to know, but heard myself inquiring nonetheless, "Why?"

"Oh . . . what I have become," he said. "What journalists have made me. Not you," he amended, believing, I suppose, that he'd insulted me. "My reputation, I mean. It stood like a wall between my family and me. I don't think they saw me. Not *me*. They saw what they believed I am."

The voice of Billy Howard made me start. "Well, why does he just *sit* there?" he said.

Clay ignored him. Or, perhaps, he did not even hear, so deep was he immersed in black thoughts.

"Hickok was right," he said, "I am not a man anymore. I'm a figment of imagination. Do you know, I looked at my reflection in the mirror this morning and did not even know who I was looking at? Who is that staring at me? I wondered. Clay Halser of Pine Grove? Or the *Hero of The Plains*?" he finished with contempt.

"*Well?*" demanded Billy Howard. "Why *does* he?"

Clay was silent for a passage of seconds and I felt my muscles drawing in, anticipating God knew what.

"I had no answer for my mirror," he went on then. "I have no answers left for anyone. All I know is that I am tired. They have offered me the job of City Marshal here and, although I could use the money, I cannot find it in myself to accept."

Clay Halser stared into my eyes and told me quietly, "To answer your long-time question: yes, Frank, I have learned what fear is. Though not fear of . . ."

He broke off as the boy spoke again, his tone now venomous. "I think he is afraid of me," said Billy Howard.

Clay drew in a long, deep breath, then slowly shifted his gaze to look across my shoulder. I sat immobile, conscious of an air of tension in the entire room now, everyone waiting with held breath.

"That is what I think," the boy's voice said. "I think Almighty God Halser is afraid of me."

Clay said nothing, looking past me at the boy. I did not dare to turn. I sat there, petrified.

"I think the Almighty God Halser is a yellow skunk!" cried Billy Howard. "I think he is a murderer who shoots men in the back and will not! . . ."

The boy's voice stopped again as Clay stood so abruptly that I felt a painful jolting in my heart. "I'll be right back," he said.

He walked past me and, shuddering, I turned to watch. It had grown so deathly still in the room that, as I did, the legs of my chair squeaked and caused some nearby diners to start.

I saw, now, for the first time, Clay Halser's challenger and was aghast at the callow look of him. He could not have been more than sixteen years of age and might well have been younger, his face speckled with skin blemishes, his dark hair long and shaggy. He was poorly dressed and had an old six-shooter pushed beneath the waistband of his faded trousers.

I wondered vaguely whether I should move, for I was sitting in whatever line of fire the boy might direct. I wondered vaguely if the other diners were wondering the same thing. If they were, their limbs were as frozen as mine.

I heard every word exchanged by the two.

"Now don't you think that we have had enough of this?" Clay said to the boy. "These folks are having their breakfast and I think that we should let them eat their meal in peace."

"Step out into the street then," said the boy.

"Now why should I step out into the street?" Clay asked. I knew it was no question. He was doing what he could to calm the agitated boy—that agitation obvious as the boy replied, "To fight me with your gun."

"You don't want to fight me," Clay informed him. "You would just be killed and no one would be better for it."

"You mean *you* don't want to fight *me*," the youth retorted. Even from where I sat, I could see that his face was almost white; it was clear that he was terror-stricken.

Still, he would not allow himself to back off, though Clay was giving him full opportunity. "*You* don't want to fight *me*," he repeated.

"That is not the case at all," Clay replied. "It is just that I am tired of fighting."

"I *thought* so!" cried the boy with malignant glee.

"Look," Clay told him quietly, "if it will make you feel good, you are free to tell your friends, or anyone you choose, that I backed down from you. You have my permission to do that."

"I don't need your d——d permission," snarled the boy. With a sudden move, he scraped his chair back, rising to feet. Unnervingly, he seemed to be gaining resolution rather than losing it—as though, in some way, he sensed the weakness in Clay, despite the fact that Clay was famous for his prowess with the handgun. "I am sick of listening to you," he declared. "Are you going to step outside with me and pull your gun like a man, or do I shoot you down like a dog?"

"*Go home*, boy," Clay responded—and I felt an icy grip of premonition strike me full force as his voice broke in the middle of a word.

"Pull, you yellow b——d," Billy Howard ordered him.

Several diners close to them lunged up from their tables, scattering for the lobby. Clay stood motionless.

"I said *pull*, you God d——d son of a b——h!" Billy Howard shouted.

"No," was all Clay Halser answered.

"Then *I* will!" cried the boy.

Before his gun was halfway from the waistband of his trousers, Clay's had cleared its holster. Then—with what capricious twist of fate!—his shot misfired and, before he could squeeze off another, the boy's gun had discharged and a bullet struck Clay full in the chest, sending him reeling back to hit a table, then sprawl sideways to the floor.

Through the pall of dark smoke, Billy Howard gaped down at his victim. "I did it," he muttered. "I *did* it." Though chance alone had done it.

Suddenly, his pistol clattered to the floor as his fingers lost their holding power and, with a cry of what he likely thought was victory, he bolted from the room. (Later, I heard, he was killed in a knife fight over a poker game somewhere near Bijou Basin.)

By then, I'd reached Clay, who had rolled onto his back, a dazed expression on his face, his right hand pressed against the blood-pumping wound in the center of his chest. I shouted for someone to get a doctor, and saw some man go dashing toward the lobby. Clay attempted to sit up, but did not have the strength, and slumped back.

Hastily, I knelt beside him and removed my coat to form a pillow underneath his head, then wedged my handkerchief between his fingers and the wound. As I did, he looked at me as though I were a stranger. Finally, he blinked and, to my startlement, began to chuckle. "The one time I di . . ." I could not make out the rest. "What, Clay?" I asked distractedly, wondering if I should try to stop the bleeding in some other way.

He chuckled again. "The one day I did not reload," he repeated with effort. "Ben would laugh at that."

179

He swallowed, then began to make a choking noise, a trickle of blood issuing from the left-hand corner of his mouth. "Hang on," I said, pressing my hand to his shoulder. "The doctor will be here directly."

He shook his head with several hitching movements. "No sawbones can remove me from *this* tight," he said.

He stared up at the ceiling now, his breath a liquid sound that made me shiver. I did not know what to say, but could only keep directing worried (and increasingly angry) glances toward the lobby. "Where *is* he?" I muttered.

Clay made a ghastly, wheezing noise, then said, "My God." His fingers closed in, clutching at the already blood-soaked handkerchief. "I am going to die." Another strangling breath. "And I am only thirty-one years old."

Instant tears distorted my vision. *Thirty-one?*

Clay murmured something I could not hear. Automatically, I bent over and he repeated, in a labored whisper, "She was such a pretty girl."

"Who?" I asked; could not help but ask.

"Mary Jane," he answered. He could barely speak by then. Straightening up, I saw the grayness of death seeping into his face and knew that there were only moments left to him.

He made a sound which might have been a chuckle had it not emerged in such a hideously bubbling manner. His eyes seemed lit now with some kind of strange amusement. "I could have married her," he managed to say. "I could still be there." He stared into his fading thoughts. "Then I would never have . . ."

At which his stare went lifeless and he expired.

I gazed at him until the doctor came. Then the two of us lifted his body—how *frail* it was—and placed it on a nearby table. The doctor closed Clay's eyes and I crossed Clay's arms on his chest after buttoning his coat across the ugly wound. Now he looked almost at peace, his expression that of a sleeping boy.

Soon people began to enter the dining room. In a short while, everyone in Silver Gulch, it seemed, had heard about Clay's death and come running to view the remains. They shuffled past his impromptu bier in a double line, gazed at him and, ofttimes, murmured some remark about his life and death.

As I stood beside the table, looking at the gray, still features, I wondered what Clay had been about to say before the rancorous voice of Billy Howard had interrupted. He'd said that he had learned what fear is, "though not fear of . . ." What words had he been about to say? Though not fear of other men? Of danger? Of death?

Later on, the undertaker came and took Clay's body after I had guaranteed his payment. That done, I was requested, by the manager of the hotel, to examine Clay's room and see to the disposal of his meager goods. This I did and will return his possessions to his family in Indiana.

With one exception.

In a lower bureau drawer, I found a stack of Record Books bound together with heavy twine. They turned out to be a journal which Clay Halser kept from the latter part of the War to this very morning.

It is my conviction that these books deserve to be published. Not in their entirety, of course; if that were done, I estimate the book would run in excess of a thousand pages. Moreover, there are many entries which, while perhaps of interest to immediate family (who will, of course, receive the Record Books when I have finished partially transcribing them), contribute nothing to the main thrust of his account, which is the unfoldment of his life as a nationally recognized lawman and gun-fighter.

Accordingly, I plan to eliminate those sections of the journal which chronicle that variety of events which any man might experience during twelve years' time. After all, as hair-raising as Clay's life was, he could not possibly exist on the razor edge of peril every day of his life. As proof of this, I will incorporate a random sampling of those entries which may be considered, from a "thrilling" standpoint, more mundane.

In this way—concentrating on the sequences of "action"—it is hoped that the general reader, who might otherwise ignore the narrative because of its unwieldy length, will more willingly expose his interest to the life of one whom another journalist has referred to as "The Prince of Pistoleers."

Toward this end, I will, additionally, attempt to make corrections in the spelling, grammar and, especially, punctuation of the journal, leaving, as an indication of this necessity, the opening entry. It goes without saying that subsequent entries need less attention to this aspect since Clay Halser learned, by various means, to read and write with more skill in his later years.

I hope the reader will concur that, while there might well be a certain charm in viewing the entries precisely as Clay Halser wrote them, the difficulty in following his style through virtually an entire book would make the reading far too difficult. It is for this reason that I have tried to simplify his phraseology without—I trust—sacrificing the basic flavor of his language.

Keep in mind, then, that if the chronology of this account is, now and then, sporadic (with occasional truncated entries), it is because I have used, as its main basis, Clay Halser's life as a man of violence. I hope, by doing this, that I will not unbalance the impression of his personality. While trying not to intrude unduly on the texture of the journal, I may occasionally break into it if I believe my observations may enable the reader to better understand the protagonist of what is probably the bloodiest sequence of events to ever take place on the American frontier.

I plan to do all this, not for personal encomiums, but because I hope that I may be the agency by which the public-at-large may come to know Clay Halser's singular story, perhaps to thrill at his exploits, perhaps to moralize but, hopefully, to profit by the reading for, through the page-by-page transition of this man from high-hearted exuberance to hopeless resignation, we may, perhaps, achieve some insight into a sad, albeit fascinating and exciting, phenomenon of our times.

Frank Leslie
April 19, 1876

If you enjoyed this book, subscribe now and get...

TWO FREE

A $7.00 VALUE—